ALSO BY MICHAEL NEWTON

MOUNTAIN DEVILS

MOUNTAIN DEVILS

GIDEON THORN
BOOK 4

MICHAEL NEWTON

Mountain Devils
Paperback Edition

Dark Wolf Books
An Imprint of Wolfpack Publishing
1707 E. Diana Street
Tampa, FL 33610

www.darkwolfbooks.com

Paperback ISBN 979-8-89567-938-8
Ebook ISBN 979-8-89567-943-2

MOUNTAIN DEVILS

PROLOGUE

SISKIYOU COUNTY, CALIFORNIA: MARCH 13, 1876

"You hear that, Swede?" Jack Hanna asked, his rough voice dropping almost to a whisper.

"I ain't deaf," Lars Linblad—"Swede" to everyone in camp—hissed in reply.

Huddled beside them, Alec Bardin muttered, "What de hell was dat?"

"You tell me, Frenchy," Hanna growled back.

"Sounded like wood knocking," Linblad offered, standing half-crouched in the chilled darkness and waiting for the sound to come again.

And there it was: a hollow *clonk*ing noise as if someone had found a fallen tree branch, nice and stout, and had decided to start drumming on a tree trunk, maybe pounding a giant sequoia or a Ponderosa pine. Positioned as they were in the deep forest, none of them could say exactly, but the resonance was there, a haunting echo in the pitch-black night, with moon and stars blocked out by looming conifers.

"How far away, you tink?" the Swede asked no one in particular.

"Can't say," Hanna replied. "Could be a hunnerd yards or half a mile."

"Closer dan dat," Bardin chimed in. "Sounds sharpish, like it ain't too far."

Hanna considered that, spat into fallen pine needles, and said, "I guess we'd better go and see."

It was the very reason they'd been set as guards, of course. Four weeks now, since the trouble started at their logging camp, with odd nocturnal noises first, then early risers waking to find things were moved around in camp or missing altogether, stout axe handles snapped in two as if a giant came around one night and broke them for the hell of it with no one noticing. That stunt had set them back two days, while their foreman went to Sacramento and retrieved more tools, together with four Henry rifles to defend their huddled bastion in the wilderness.

Most of the men in camp had started out blaming the Yuroks, who opposed encroachment on their hunting grounds, but when the county sheriff visited their village, all the tribesmen made a show of wide-eyed innocence, citing some ancient heathen legend as the cause behind it all. Jack Hanna didn't even try to follow that part of their argument. Tonight, assigned to lead the guard detail, he'd drawn one of the Henrys, leaving Swede to take a double-barreled shotgun, Frenchy settling for a pistol he had brought to camp from God knew where.

The three of them, Hanna supposed, could handle anything they might discover in the midnight woods, be it a Yurok pulling pranks, a grizzly craving meat after its winter's sleep, or anything the forest chose to throw against them.

Knock-knock-knock. A heavy, rhythmic sound that let you know it wasn't just some dangling limb stirred by the breeze, but a deliberate hammering. A conscious choice, almost a *signal*, now he thought about it. And it had to be a big man doing it, no pint-sized shrimp with wizened arms.

"C'mon with me," he told the others, finally asserting his command.

"You mean dat?" French asked him, not quite challenging.

"I said it, didn't I?"

"We don't know who it *is,*" Linblad reminded him.

"That's why we're out here, damn it!"

"Or *how many* there could be."

As if in answer to that thought, the knocking sounded from a new direction, off to Hanna's left, northwestward. It was answered almost instantly by the first sound they'd heard, due north this time, or straight ahead from where he stood. And not an echo, either: they were clear, distinct, and separate sounds. No single man could duplicate that drumming give-and-take all by himself. It was impossible.

"At least two of 'em, then," Hanna allowed. "We'll have to separate and run 'em down."

"*Merde,*" Frenchy swore. "I don't like dat."

"No sir," the Swede agreed.

"You listen up!" snapped Hanna. "This shit has to stop. It's why we're out here, drawin' overtime, and I ain't slinkin' back to camp, tellin' Ed Russell I got scairt of knockin' in the dark."

Ed was their foreman, six feet seven inches tall and every bit of it hard-charging muscle, not afraid of anything from falling timber to a raging forest fire, with fists the size of fattened roasting hens.

"*Mère Mary,*" the Frenchman muttered. Then, reluctantly, "I go with you."

"Why not?" Linblad chimed in. "We have the guns."

"Don't be afraid to use 'em, neither," Hanna said. "Just make damn sure you don't shoot *me*."

Lars Linblad was accustomed to the cold from his homeland, now half a world away. It might be two nights shy of spring, according to the calendar, but there was still snow on the ground in northern California and might be for another month, unless the weather turned. They were three nights past the full moon, and while its light had bathed their camp on Friday night, its fading remnant was completely lost in virgin forest after sundown, where the great old trees still loomed between a hundred and two hundred feet above the tallest man.

While they survived, that is.

Axes and saws were coming for them, sure as God made sun and wind and rain. None would escape, if Ed Russell and those who'd hired him had their way.

Linblad gave little thought to what came after that, when they had clear-cut everything in sight. He wasn't paid to think, just use his muscle to achieve the boss man's goal, whatever that may be. If Congress and the State of California didn't mind—

Knock-knock!

He clutched the Remington tightly enough to make his knuckles ache, despite the numbness that had crept into his hands inside stout leather gloves. It was a twelve-gauge double-barrel, and the pockets of his long coat bulged with extra cartridges. Linblad stopped short of thumbing back the weapon's hammers when the knocking startled him, and that was good, because the index finger of his right hand was already curled inside the trigger guard.

He didn't have to ask the others if they'd heard the sound. Hanna was slinking forward with his rifle shouldered, Frenchy Bardin using both hands to control his trembling six-gun as he followed on their leader's heels. That made Linblad the last man in line, and he picked up his pace, to keep from being left behind.

The knocking sounds repeated, forcing them to stop and scan the darkness that surrounded them. This time, it sounded as if there were three distinct and separate sources for the booming, rhythmic noise—including one somewhere behind Linblad, between him and the logging camp, that made him mutter, "*Söta Jesus,* we're surrounded!"

"Hush back there," Hanna commanded, in a voice that brooked no argument.

Linblad wondered if anyone in camp—where three more guards were standing watch while his crew roamed the woods—could hear the booming noise that echoed in his ears. They sounded louder than artillery from where he stood, but some of that, he understood, was fear swiftly progressing into panic. Linblad vowed that he would not desert his comrades, but in realistic terms, how long could he control the terror that he felt inside?

In fact, it only mattered for a few more seconds.

The attack came from his left, a rushing sound like winter wind amid the trees, and he was swept completely off his feet by something that collided with him, literally scooped him off his size-eleven boots, and carried him away in what he took for massive, crushing arms. Those arms clutched him so tightly that his own felt numb. Linblad's right hand would not obey the order flashing from his startled brain, to cock and fire the shotgun now, before it was too late. His bearded cheek pressed close against something like leather underlain with bulging muscle, fringed by fur that bore an odor rank and nearly nauseating.

Linblad half imagined someone calling out his name, as from a distance or beyond a yawning void. His final conscious act, before the darkness claimed him, was to answer back—a squeak more than a cry for help—then something snapped inside him, near the juncture of his skull and neck.

Incredibly, he clung to life somehow and would regret it soon.

The night had something vastly worse in store for him than being paralyzed.

"Swede?" Alec Bardin called out into the chilly darkness. "Where'n hell is you?"

No answer came from Linblad, but Jack Hanna doubled back to join the Frenchman, Henry rifle held across his chest as if it might protect him from a sudden blow. "What's goin' on back here?" he growled.

"The Swede's gone," Bardin said, his wide eyes probing at the night. "I heard somethin' an he was gone."

"Heard *what?*" Hanna demanded.

"I can't answer dat," Bardin replied. "Somethin' like runnin' feet, and den an 'oof' noise an he gone."

"What kinda noise was that?"

"*Oof!*" Bardin emphasized. "Like somethin' knock de wind right outa 'im."

"That's crazy talk, Frenchy."

"So where he at, den?"

"How'n hell should *I* know? You were closer to 'im."

"An I tell you what I hear. You don't wanna believe it, that's your—"

An ungodly scream cut off Bardin's reply. He might have said it was an animal howling, but there was something human in the ringing sound that made his skin crawl. "*Merde!* Is dat de Swede?"

"How could it be?" Hanna shot back. "It sounds like—"

"Somethin' killin' 'im," Frenchy cut in.

Hanna considered that and said, "We need to split up, just in case."

"You crazy, man, or what?"

"We're gonna flank the sound and find out what'n hell it is."

At least they'd have no trouble tracking it. As Hanna spoke, another scream rang out, immediately followed by another and another, each one louder, *wetter* than the last.

"We best be gettin' back to camp for *renforts,*" Bardin said.

"Speak English, will ya? What's that mean?"

"The reinforcements. Men and guns."

Hanna seemed to consider it, then shook his head. "We got a job to do. Let's get 'er done."

Mouthing a silent string of vile obscenities, Bardin saw to his weapon. It was a LeMat revolver, manufactured by a Frenchman in New Orleans early in America's great Civil War. Its cylinder held nine .42-caliber rounds and revolved around a larger .60-caliber barrel for birdshot, the equivalent of a single-shot twenty-gauge shotgun. Reports claimed it was devastating at close range, though Bardin had not slain a living thing with it since he acquired the weapon two years earlier.

Now, it might save his life—or blow up in his face.

Which, he supposed, was better than whatever caused the Swede to scream that way.

Reluctantly, he parted company with Hanna, veering off a few yards to his left in an attempt to flank the screaming man concealed by darkness, somewhere up ahead. He almost hoped the screams would end and leave them without any point of reference to follow in the forest, but in fact they seemed to multiply, growing progressively more hideous until a soggy *ripping* sound abruptly cut off the pathetic wails.

That froze the Frenchman in his tracks for just a moment, but he forced himself to plod ahead, Hanna already lost to sight amid the darkness and the looming conifers. Frenchy wished he had passed on logging when he had the chance and gone out on a fishing boat from San Francisco. That way, all he'd have to fret about was drowning, maybe being eaten by a shark. But this...

More ripping, rending sounds, and Bardin forced himself forward, cranking back the hammer on his thirteen-inch revolver, nearly three and a half pounds of metal with all its chambers loaded and ready to fire. He thought he'd lead off with the birdshot, powerful enough to rock a man at forty yards, though not to kill him outright. That should daze whatever he was firing at and give him time to pepper it with his .42-caliber slugs and do some fatal damage.

All he needed was a fighting chance, and—

When the giant hand clamped over Frenchy's face, occluding both his nose and mouth from drawing any further breath, he triggered the LeMat by accident, spraying the forest night with leaden shot. Was that a cry of pain he heard? He fervently hoped so, then wondered who or what he might have wounded.

Fingers fatter than cigars, thicker than *falukorv* sausage, tightened around his lower face and squeezed. Bones cracked, teeth lost their moorings in his gums, and in another moment Alec Bardin found himself drowning in his own blood.

The birdshot struck Jack Hanna from behind, lacing his lower back, buttocks and thighs with stabbing pain. He stumbled, dropped to hands and knees, doing his best to turn and raise the Henry rifle he had nearly lost while falling.

"Frenchy!" he raged into darkness. "Did you shoot me, damn your eyes?"

Bardin did not reply, although Jack thought he heard a grappling sound of struggle somewhere in the night, off to his left. There was a grunting, wheezing sound like something dying hard, but no more gunshots, and he couldn't tell if that was Bardin crossing over, or if he'd managed to kill whatever they were looking for.

Not likely, after shooting me, thought Hanna. Still, he called out, "Frenchy! Are you there!"

And once again, no answer.

Streaming curses now under his breath, Hanna knew it was time to rethink what had passed for strategy since they left camp with orders to go hunting whatever it was that prowled the woods by night. He was alone now, and scared spitless if he told God's honest truth about it. Standing in the cold dark with the Henry rifle trembling in his hands and not a target anywhere in sight.

But there was movement in among the trees, oh yes. Just take your pick of heavy plodding sounds, harsh breathing from a set of lungs that must be big as bellows, or the ugly dripping noise that could be anything but smelled too much like blood for Hanna's taste. He'd spent a teenage summer in a slaughterhouse and knew that stench all right, though he'd managed to dodge the wartime draft by coming west and never had to smell it on a battlefield.

Hanna had killed his share of animals but hadn't shot a man so far, if that was what—or *who*—was making all the noise surrounding him right now. He hoped not, since the size of any man like that would have been terrifying in its own right, without any racket in the night to help. It barely calmed him, knowing that his Henry had a full load of sixteen .44 rounds in its magazine and one in the chamber, ready to fly. Now he was scared *and* wounded, being armed for bear was no great reassurance in itself.

Go back, he thought. *Get help like Frenchy wanted to before. Just get the hell away from here!*

Jack fixed his mental compass on the logging camp and took his first step back in that direction, feeling just a trifle better once he'd made that move. Okay, he had a mile or so to travel through the dark, but still...

The noises started moving right along with him, as if a pack of wolves was stalking him, but these would have to be the grandpa giant wolves of any seen by man since the beginning of recorded time. Those footsteps, heavy breathing, crackling in the undergrowth, all spoke of *size* and *weight* beyond the scope of any forest-dwelling creature he could name, except a grizzly bear, but grizzlies didn't hunt in packs—did they?

But Christ, he almost wished they *did,* which would be

something he could understand at least, instead of...what, some monster from a nightmare come to life?

Hanna put one boot down before the other, clocking off the yards, eyes sweeping sterile darkness for whatever might be stalking him. He didn't look for Frenchy or the Swede, was frankly terrified of what he might discover if he found them, focused solely on the goal of getting back to camp, beside a fire, and rallying the other men into a search party.

If he could just—

The charge came from behind him, rushing up on Hanna's blind side. He was quick enough to turn and fire a wild shot from his Henry, *crack*ing in the night, then pump the rifle's lever-action down and back, reloading it, before *another* adversary hit him from the left, with all the force Hanna imagined that a freight train might impart.

He fell, sprawling, but kept his tight grip on the Henry, pivoting around on legs that didn't work exactly right to fire a second shot. He actually had a target that time, huge and looming from the darker shadows that surrounded it, with red eyes glinting far above him, maybe eight or nine feet off the forest floor that cushioned him with fallen needles from the evergreens.

Before Hanna could fire again, great hands descended on him from behind—his second enemy, perhaps a third—clenching his shoulders hard enough to crack his collar-bones and make him scream as he was lifted effortlessly, spun around, and flung into the night.

Where something else caught him as if it had been planned that way, drawing him toward a gaping mouth replete with long, curved fangs waiting to tear his throat open before another scream escaped.

Jack Hanna's last thought was that he had failed, for once, to do his job.

ONE

SACRAMENTO, CALIFORNIA: APRIL 18, 1876

Gideon Thorn had passed his birthday on the trail, turned twenty-four on his last night camped out in the Sierra Nevada Mountains, before he started his descent into the Sacramento Valley. The name translated from its Spanish roots as "sacrament" or "means of grace," but nothing quite so calm and peaceful drew him there.

Thorn was continuing a quest that had begun when he was two years old, to find an honest explanation for the slaughter of his family in what was then a part of Kansas Territory, split off into Colorado Territory seven years later, with the nation poised for civil war. He hadn't started seeking answers then, of course: first came the orphanage, then rescue by his wealthy Aunt Drusilla in the person of her manservant—Obi Magoro, a unique and wholly unexpected African. Then followed school in Boston, where he'd learned to face down bullies with Magoro's help, and Harvard University, where Thorn had graduated *summa cum laude* at twenty-one, earmarked for law school in the autumn of 1873.

But life had other plans for Thorn. His aunt's death that summer, bequeathing him most of her fortune, had opened a new world for Gideon in the Wild West. Somewhere, he'd reasoned, there *must* be an answer to the murders of his parents and his elder brother, passed off by a lazy sheriff as an animal attack of unknown origin. And the fact he hadn't found that answer yet, as he began the third year of his quest, dismayed Thorn not at all.

Sacramento had been named as California's capital in 1854, the year Thorn's family was massacred and seven years after John Sutter launched the valley's agricultural industry by planting two thousand fruit trees. Gold had followed orchards, with the strike at Sutter's Mill in 1848, launching a population boom that brought ten thousand residents of all kinds to the city. A devastating flood and cholera epidemic in 1850 failed to break the city's spirit, and census takers counted more than sixteen thousand residents in 1870. A year before that tabulation, the First Continental Railroad had linked Sacramento to the distant East and all points in between.

Thorn had considered traveling by rail from his last stop in Colorado, but decided he would rather take his time and see more of the country riding westward on his stallion, Shadow, trailing pack mule Bell behind over mountains, desert, then more mountains, down into the valley some were hailing as a Paradise on Earth. He wasn't sure if that shoe fit—ten miles due east of town he'd passed two bodies hanging from a stout oak tree, branded as bandits by the cardboard signs around their necks—but it was certainly a change.

And would it bring him to the end of his long journey, if indeed there was an end to reach?

Thorn reckoned he would have to wait and see.

His first stop in the capital had been the Sacramento Arms Hotel, downtown on K Street, where he'd booked a room and hauled his personal effects upstairs. From there, he found a livery stable four blocks distant, sized it up, and finally decided he could trust his animals to the old hostler with a ready smile and twinkle in his one good eye. He'd seen them settled, left them with a silent message of encouragement—a talent from his youth, communicating mentally with so-called "lesser" species—then moved on to get the lay of Sacramento for himself.

Thorn made a striking figure on the street, drawing attention from the locals as he passed and stopped to browse at shop windows along the way. Clad all in black from hat to boots, except the white shirt underneath his vest, he measured six foot four and wore a pair of Colt Peacemakers on his hips, tied down. A twelve-inch Bowie knife was sheathed behind his back, the pommel of a smaller dagger rising from its scabbard on the outside of his tall right boot. When Thorn took off his hat, as in a restaurant, eyes naturally were attracted to the white streak in his ebon hair, running from hairline to the crown.

A souvenir of his last night as anybody's son, constant reminder of the talon that had marked him as a two-year-old but still permitted him to live.

The *why* of that was one question that drove him on, hoping his next stop, or the next one after that, would tell him that much, anyway, and partially release him from the mystery that haunted him by day and night.

Perhaps in California, if the stories he had heard were true...

The only shop where Thorn spent any of his money on that first day in the capital was a peculiar store on Eighth Street, near a park, that seemed to specialize in curiosities. Its stock included shrunken heads from the South Seas, Indian artifacts retrieved throughout the West, and taxidermy specimens prepared by someone who had caught the knack of making reptiles, rodents, and some larger species seem alive in death.

None of those got his coins, however. Thorn's two purchases were small and made of silver: one a simulated eagle's feather, and the other a dime-sized mandala common to the Eastern faiths of Buddhism and Hinduism. He shelled out a dollar each and added them to the collection worn around his neck, suspended from a silver chain: a cross, a Star of David, Islam's crescent, and a pentagram for paganism.

Thorn had never been religious in the normal sense. Rather, he chose to take the best of what he found from various belief systems and left the rest behind—their biases, constraints on personal behavior and free will, insistence that a certain hide-bound dogma was the only "One True Way."

The extra weight around his neck was slight, and somehow comforting.

He'd covered all the bases, as his baseball coach at Harvard might have said.

Reginald Conklin was a man of means; *significant,* he might have said, should modesty permit it. At the very least, he was a mover in the economic world of Northern California, known in Sacramento and in San Francisco too, a name mentioned as far south as Los Angeles when conversation turned to logging, lumber, and related industries.

At forty-one, he was vice president of operations for Siskiyou Logging, tasked by his employer with ensuring that big timber fed the local mills nonstop, in turn supplying boards, plywood, and paper pulp to buyers ranging from the Golden State to Kansas City in Missouri, south as far as Phoenix, Dallas, and New Orleans on the Gulf of Mexico. It would be no exaggeration to observe that several million dollars hinged on his efficiency each year.

But lately, that fabled efficiency had been...impaired.

It angered Conklin even to consider it, curdled the breakfast in his stomach on this Tuesday morning, and inclined him to be snappish around his subordinates, or strangers who approached him with some inquiry Conklin found tedious. He'd earned a reputation during recent weeks for snapping at his secretary, foremen, and a host of other underlings around headquarters in the capital, and out among the forests where he'd once turned giant living trees into a kind of gold.

For that, he blamed the Yurok tribe exclusively. Peaceful by most accounts, they'd thrown a major monkey wrench into his works with fables, muttered threats, and incidents that had his rough, tough loggers quaking in their boots, ready to find another trade or stretch of forest to denude. A few of them had landed in their graves, while local law enforcement shrugged, threw up its hands, and pleaded impotence.

Now Conklin had a plan in mind to fix all that, and if it worked out well, he just might turn a tidy profit on the side. But if he failed...well, starting over would be difficult at his age, and he had no realistic hope at all of moving laterally to another logging company.

Not after he had done his best and seen it come to naught.

Distracted as he was, Conklin did not notice the three young men approaching him on K Street, three blocks from his office. When he spotted them, too late, he saw the seedy look they shared, an air of having drunk the night away, and something like rapacious hunger in their bloodshot eyes. All three were armed: one with a pistol tucked under his belt, the other two with long knives sheathed on theirs.

"Hey, Mister, how ya doin'?" asked the gunman of the group, when they had closed to ten or fifteen feet.

"Fine, thank you," Conklin said, and moved to step around them, but the trio fanned out just enough to block his path entirely.

"Them's nice duds," one of the others said, hand resting on the pommel of his knife.

"Look like they cost you dear," the third one said.

Before Conklin could think of a response, the gunman said, "Rich fella like yourself, I bet you wouldn't mind helpin' the poorly out a bit. Us three, for instance."

"No," said Conklin, cutting through their beggars' pitch.

"That's it?" the seeming leader of the trio asked. "Just 'no'?"

Conklin could recognize the danger those three posed for him, but he was getting angry, too, his famous temper taking over.

"Which part of the answer I supplied confuses you?" he asked the thugs as one.

"That sounds like lip to me," one of the knife men said, half-smiling. "Snotty rich man's lip, supposed to make us feel all small and sorry for ourselves."

"Don't make me feel that way," the gunman said. "Either o' you boys feel like that?"

"Not me," the third replied. "Truth is, it makes me fightin' mad."

"No reason I can think of," said the second, "we don't *take* whatever Grandpa here has on him and be done with it."

"Well," said the gunman, "we *did* ask him, all nice and polite."

Conklin had drawn himself up to his full height, five foot ten, and clenched his fists. He wished that he was carrying a walking stick—or better yet, a sword cane—but he was unarmed save for a small penknife in his right trouser pocket, which he'd never reach in time.

"You plan to rob me in broad daylight, on a public street?" he challenged them.

"Don't see why not," the gunman said, craning his neck this way and that as if in search of witnesses or lawmen on patrol.

"O'course," the second one suggested, "if you wanna hand the money over nice and peaceful like..."

"And don't forget that pocket watch," said Number Three.

"I'll give you nothing," Conklin blustered. "And the three of you can go to hell."

"I'm bettin' that you get there well ahead of us," the gunman said, hand rising for the first time toward the curved grip of his weapon. Conklin noted, also for the first time, that the pistol's grip had three deep notches etched into its walnut handle. Conklin knew his wood, but hoped those notches didn't stand for three men dead.

"Now, are you gonna hand it over," asked the gunman, "or—"

Another man's voice interrupted him, saying, "You might want to think twice about that move."

Thorn rose early, force of habit, and was second to arrive at the Sacramento Arms's restaurant for breakfast, after a roly-poly businessman who could have been an illustration for the term "stuffed shirt." A young but weary-looking waitress brought his menu, filled his mug with hot black coffee, and departed while he scanned the morning's offerings.

There was a lot to choose from, but he finally decided on simplicity: fried eggs with ham, a half grapefruit provided with its own small spoon, and buttermilk pancakes wit maple syrup on the side. Before his meal arrived, a few more hotel guests appeared to start their day with something savory or sweet. Each new arrival seemed to pause while passing by his table, as they gaped at Thorn's streak of white hair rising above his lean, young face, but none was déclassé enough to comment on the stripe—at least, within his hearing.

Go ahead and have your look, he thought. *I see it every living day.*

When he had finished, charged his breakfast to the room and left the waitress a sufficient tip, Thorn plucked his black hat from the chair beside him and concealed his strange badge of survival for another stroll downtown. He had a goal in mind, already scouted yesterday, when he'd arrived, but still had no appointment for a meeting with the man he meant to see.

Too bad. He'd think of something when the time came, or he'd wait around outside the red brick office block and spot the subject of his interest as he emerged around midday. A portrait of him from the *Sacramento Bee,* published some weeks ago, was trapped and frozen in

Thorn's photographic memory—another handy trait he shared with being ambidextrous and communicating mentally with animals.

The very last thing Thorn expected, as he left the Sacramento Arms, was to observe his target standing less than two blocks south of the hotel just then, beside what seemed to be the entrance to a narrow alleyway. The subject's progress down the sidewalk had been interrupted by three shady looking characters in baggy shirts and drooping trousers, two of them with hats atop their heads at angles doubtless meant to grace them with a rakish air.

Their backs were turned to Thorn as he approached them casually, but he had a clear view of his target's reddened, worried-looking face. There was some kind of hostile confrontation underway, and while Thorn missed the greater part of it, no psychic powers were required to recognize some kind of mugging being perpetrated in broad daylight, seemingly without fear of police arriving on the scene.

Perhaps the three were drunk. Just now, Thorn neither knew nor cared.

He came up from behind them, just in time to hear one say, "Now, are you gonna hand it over, or-"

"You might want to think twice about that move," Thorn interrupted him.

Three faces whipped around to glare at him, the fourth —his friend to be, with any luck—staring past them, regarding Thorn with curiosity and, possibly, another hint of dread.

"The hell are you?" one of the thugs demanded, softening his face a little when his eyes dipped to behold Thorn's twin Peacemakers, tied down to facilitate a rapid draw.

"I might ask you the same," Thorn said. "Thing is, I really just don't care."

"You shouldn't mess with us," the trio's spokesman said. He had a cheap and smallish pistol tucked into his belt. The other two were packing knives.

"Not my intention, I assure you," Thorn replied, smiling. "I'm simply asking you to let this gentleman go on about his business, while you three tend to yours."

"He *is* our bidness," said a second of the three, fingers encircling the handle of his knife. Thorn couldn't say if it would be a Bowie or an Arkansas toothpick, but neither matched a bullet when it came to speed.

A quick move from his thumbs released the hammer thongs on Gideon's revolvers. All three of his adversaries saw it, wearing different shapes of scowl, but Thorn kept smiling as he said, "Then I suppose we have a problem here."

"I doubt you can take three of us," their mouthpiece said.

Thorn shrugged, hands near his guns, and answered, "Stranger things have happened, though."

The would-be robbers pondered that while Thorn edged slightly to his left, getting a better angle on the trio if he had to draw and fire both Colts at once. Above all else, he didn't want to wound their pigeon in the process if he could avoid it. That would seriously put a damper on the conversation he still hoped to have with their intended victim, once this sidewalk drama had been swept aside.

So far, there'd been no hostile moves, and Thorn hoped that he could defuse the situation, at least slightly, if he turned his mind to it. Still smiling like a man without a worry in the world, he said, "You boys look like you've had a hard night. Maybe hard lives all along, but I don't know and

I don't care. You're making a mistake right now. Consider how your lives will turn if you do something stupid now and wind up crippled. Or I might just kill you. Then you'd have no lives at all."

"Big talk," one of them said, before the pistolero slapped an open hand against his chest and snarled, "Shut up, Jed." Then, to Thorn, "I think we'll just be goin' now."

"A wise decision," Thorn answered, and stood aside to let them pass, watching them on their way in case they tried a sneak attack.

"My God!" his target said. "That was a marvelous display, Mister...?"

"Gideon Thorn."

They shook hands, with the older man's grip trembling slightly as he introduced himself. "Reginald Conklin, sir."

"I know," Thorn said. "You're just the man I've come to see."

TWO

"I beg your pardon. Did you say—?"

"That I'm in town to meet you," Thorn replied. "Precisely, Mr. Conklin."

"But—"

"It's with regard to your impending expedition from Yreka," Thorn pressed on. "The so-called monster hunt."

Conklin was frowning now. "That greatly oversimplifies the matter, Mr. Thorn." Running his eyes over Thorn's frame and holstered guns, he added, "I would not have taken you for a reporter, sir."

"Nor should you," Thorn replied. "I've known some in my time, but never wrote a word for publication and I don't expect to."

"Oh? Then why the interest in my expedition?"

"It's a matter from my private history," Thorn said. "Whether your search pertains to that or not, I couldn't say. From what I've read—"

"The *newspapers*." Conklin took no pains to conceal his personal contempt. "One mention of the so-called *Omah* and their yellow journalists go wild. It's a disgrace, I tell you!"

"But a matter you've determined to resolve."

"In my own way, if any resolution is attainable."

"That's what I hope to speak with you about," said Thorn.

Conklin withdrew a gold watch from his vest pocket and checked the time. "Unfortunately, I'm already running late for an appointment, Mr. Thorn." His face softened a bit as he added, "But in recognition of the service you've performed for me this morning, I'd be happy to discuss the matter with you. Over dinner, say? Tonight. My expedition's leaving—"

"In the morning," Thorn finished his thought for him. "Yes, sir. I know."

"Perhaps at dinner, then? Are you familiar with a restaurant called *L'rotissarie français*? It's quite the novelty, I understand. On L Street?"

"I can find it," Thorn replied.

"Shall we say seven, then? We'll share our stories."

Nodding, Thorn said, "I'll be there."

"And in the meantime, please accept my thanks for... everything."

"My pleasure, Mr. Conklin."

Thorn watched him retreat, satisfied for the moment with his introduction to Conklin. The man might have a business meeting on his calendar, but he'd also be thinking about Thorn's interest in the expedition Conklin had arranged, starting tomorrow morning from the capital as luck would have it.

Luck, and Thorn's determination to make contact in advance.

He had the better part of ten hours to fill before their

dinner meeting, and Thorn started out by finding *L'rotissarie français*. He spotted it after he'd walked nine blocks of O Street, sized it up as someplace where most of his weapons would be better left at home—or, rather, at the Sacramento Arms—and then went off to check on Bell and Shadow at the livery where he had left them overnight.

The animals were fine, and Thorn assured them without speaking that their tenure at the stable would be brief. Another night, at most, and they were heading north. Whether they did it as a part of Conklin's expedition or as separate camp followers remained to be determined after he sat down with Conklin at the restaurant to plead his case.

But either way, they would be following the hunters' trail.

Thorn's first hint of the expedition had arrived as most of his investigations had begun, by newspaper. He'd finished off a case in Colorado—missing persons whom, as it turned out, had disappeared from Breckenridge around the time strange lights were spotted in the autumn sky—without an answer pleasing either to himself or the authorities who had permitted him to snoop around after admitting they were baffled. No one vanished from the mining town while Thorn was there, nor were the eerie lights reported after he arrived. People *had* disappeared, that much was verified six ways from Sunday, but it seemed the plague had passed on by the time Thorn showed his face in town.

So he had come away dissatisfied, disgruntled, and was drifting farther westward on a whim, at loose ends, when he'd read of Conklin's trouble in a newspaper he had picked up in Reno, Nevada. The Siskiyou Logging Company—Reginald Conklin vice president of operations—had suffered losses of equipment and employees near a small town called Yreka. Some suspected Yurok Indians at work, though they'd been peaceful in the past. Others, including Yurok shamans, said a "mountain devil" had arisen to curtail destruction of their forests by the white loggers.

A mountain devil called *Omah*.

Thorn didn't recognize the native name, and browsing through the stacks of Sacramento's library had not enlightened him. He'd boned up on back issues of the *Bee,* acquired more details via word of mouth at a saloon the night before he met Conklin, but still was only burdened with the basics. Conklin and his company denied any reports of monsters on the prowl, but for their workers' peace of mind—and, Thorn suspected, with an eye toward casting blame upon the Yuroks—Conklin had an *Omah*-hunting expedition organized, including government officials in the persons of a State Department officer and someone from the grand Smithsonian museums in Washington, D.C.

Thorn planned to be among them, or at least observing from a cautious distance, when they struck off for Yreka and environs in the morning. As to what they'd find, if anything...well, that was anybody's guess.

Monsters were *real.* Thorn knew that much from personal experience, whether you meant the human kind that killed and mutilated others of their kind for sport, or creatures that were plucked out of a nightmare and dropped into daily life. He'd seen both kinds during his long, far-ranging travels through the West, and while most of his cases had a simple, down-to-Earth solution in the end, some challenged his imagination and a few, like Breckenridge, might never be resolved.

He could but try, and no one yet had ever talked him out of it.

Reginald Conklin would not be the first.

Reginald Conklin's ears weren't burning as he neared his office on K Street, but he could not deny his mind was working overtime. The scheduled meeting wasn't that important—someone had discovered pilferage at the Siskiyou warehouse and he'd be letting two of his employees go this morning, maybe pressing charges—but his present thoughts were split between his near-mugging in broad daylight, his rescue by a total stranger in the nick of time, and learning that his providential savior had been looking for him all along, intent on picking Conklin's brain about tomorrow's expedition to the northern wilderness.

Gideon Thorn looked like a normal sort of individual, despite an air of danger that he carried in his eyes and in the matched pistols he wore. There was a Bowie knife as well, Conklin had noted, and a dagger in his boot, more weapons than the average cowboy carried on a cattle drive, much less a seeming gentleman in downtown Sacramento. Looking at him, seeing how Thorn put the drunken hooligans to flight, Conklin had no doubt he was capable of violence, yet oddly did not judge him as a person to avoid.

Not yet.

Thorn had alluded to his "private history," a hint that it might overlap Conklin's dilemma in some way still undefined. Conklin would get that information from him over dinner at *L'rotissarie français,* but in the meantime there was digging to be done. Before they started breaking bread, he wanted to know everything he could find out about this young man who had saved him from a robbery and beating, maybe worse. There was a hint of Boston in his voice, and that could be a starting point. Inquiries could be made by telegraph; answers, even if they were incomplete, could be received before the hour of seven struck that evening.

And if his guess was wrong about Thorn's point of origin...then what? Conklin believed himself to be a fairly decent judge of character—what thriving businessman was not?—and he had not sized Thorn up as a rank confidence man working a dodge. There was no money to be made by asking about Conklin's expedition, though the lumberman would still play his own cards close to the vest.

Success, of course, would be a different matter altogether. If the ancient fairy tales were true and they could actually find an *Omah*, gun it down or capture it alive, there might indeed be cash enough to go around. Perhaps more than he stood to earn from Siskiyou that year—enough, in fact, to set Reg Conklin up for life.

Pipe dreams, he thought, scowling as he approached the entrance to his office building. Myths and legends didn't come to life in this eighth decade of the nineteenth century, caught up in the beginning of what politicians and reporters liked to call an Industrial Revolution. Conklin wasn't sure about all that, but he knew damn well that America was *growing* and it needed timber to expand: to build its homes and shops; to print its books and newspapers; for writing laws and binding them in statute books to rule over the hoi polloi who did the grunt work nationwide.

Siskiyou Logging was a major force to reckon with in that regard, though it could lose a fortune and its standing in the industry if workers in its forest camps were paralyzed by fear of the unknown. Conklin, in charge of operations for the company, could not permit that to occur. He was too old to find another comparable post with any decent company, would have to start from scratch among the younger men who had their eyes fixed on success, knives honed for cutting any deadwood in their way.

Starting tomorrow, bright and early, Conklin would devote himself to finding this ridiculous *Omah* or proving that the beast of legend was, in fact, nothing but smoke unfurling from a Yurok shaman's pipe. As for the murder of his loggers, that would be avenged, whether he found a way to use the law or was compelled to handle it himself.

An angry pack of miners might do that much for him, and if not, he could hire Pinkertons. The Eye That Never Sleeps had countless gunmen on its payroll who would do whatever was required of them, regardless of legality.

He hoped it wouldn't come to that in California, but Conklin was prepared to do whatever was required to keep his job and reputation as they were. And who could say? If he surprised himself and found a monster, something to upset historians and change the course of modern evolutionary theory, it might even bring advancement. Cash aside, he knew the president of Siskiyou was getting on in years, ailing as well, and who would better serve as his replacement in a year or two, than someone who had saved the company while rewriting the world's great science books?

Too much to hope for?

Not if *Omah* lived and breathed somewhere around Yreka, stalking human prey, and Conklin found a way to deal with it. He'd be a hero in the newspapers and in the boardroom, where a red-ink deluge was averted through his efforts and the firm rolled on to victory, including headlines coast to coast.

Something to shoot for.

At the very least, he'd solve a brutal spate of crimes and clinch his own position in the bargain.

And that just might be enough for now.

L'rotissarie français was going strong when Thorn arrived, five minutes early for his dinner meeting with Reginald Conklin. It felt strange, walking around the capital without his gunbelt on, but Thorn was not unarmed. He had the dagger in his boot, passed over at first glance by most who might be watching him approach the restaurant, and even if he'd left it in his hotel room, he would be more than simply capable of self-defense.

As the runty orphan boy at Boston's Weatherford Academy, marked as a victim for his age, his circumstances, and the white streak running through his jet-black hair, Thorn had been singled out for bullying by other, older boys. He'd come back home to Aunt Drusilla's stately home with cuts and bruises more than once, until Obi Magoro schooled him in the native martial arts of Africa: Dambe bare-knuckle boxing, Engolo ritual combat, and Nguni stick-fighting. The first time he'd fought back and won, it meant a summons from the headmaster, but Aunt Drusilla took no prisoners. After reminding Weatherford's administration of her fat donations to the school—which might dry up at any moment—she had mused about the possibility of litigation against teachers who permitted such harassment of her undersized nephew.

Gideon wasn't undersized for long, however. After beating down a few of his tormentors, he'd discovered school athletics and had found a happy balance between physical exertion and his academic duties. By the time he saw the last of Weatherford, he'd been adept at track and field, football and baseball—sports he carried on to Harvard while maintaining straight "As" in academia.

A snooty-looking *maître d'* looked down his nose at Gideon until Thorn told him he was meeting Mr. Conklin at the restaurant. That brought about a subtle change in attitude, the pompous ass conveying him without further delay to Conklin's booth, where he found Conklin working on a glass of wine. Once he was seated, yet another waiter brought menus and took their orders: *bœuf bourguignon* for Conklin, *coq au vin* for Thorn.

After the waiter left, Conklin wasted no time in getting down to business. "So, what is it that you want to know about my expedition?" he inquired.

Thorn answered with a question of his own. "How can I join?"

That seemed to startle Conklin. He was silent for a moment, then said, "I'm afraid we've booked the personnel we need, so you must see—"

"There's no more room in northern California?" Thorn cut him off, smiling. "Come on. You know better than that."

A trace of color showed in Conklin's cheeks before he said, "I must be honest with you, Mr. Thorn. Today, I sent inquiries to the East and I've learned quite a bit about you in the meantime."

"I'm an open book," said Thorn.

"And what a book! Orphaned at two, in some kind of disaster. The authorities blamed animals."

"*One* animal," said Gideon, correcting him.

"All right. Adopted by your wealthy aunt, a star at school, including Harvard—no mean feat—but on your way to law school you discarded all of it to...what? Roam aimlessly around the West, a vagabond?"

"Not quite," Thorn said. "Most vagabonds are penniless. I pay my own way."

"So I understand. You were your aunt's sole beneficiary."

"Not quite."

"Ah, well. The African, of course, but—"

"My best friend. The sort of man you'll likely never meet."

"Well, be that as it may, what makes you suitable for such an undertaking as I've planned? In short, why should I take you on as baggage when the roster is already filled?"

"First, I solve mysteries," Thorn said. "It won't be covered in whatever dossiers your people searched, but for the past two years and change, it's all I do."

"When you say 'mysteries'..."

"I mean exactly that: unanswered questions, deaths and disappearances, whatever. As to motive, that's my own business."

"And my guess is that it goes back to your parents, when you were a child."

"I'm still working on that one."

"And you think my quest may be somehow related to your own?"

Thorn shrugged at that, just as their food arrived. His chicken braised in wine with mushrooms, garlic, and pork fat was perfect. Conklin's beef, wine-cooked with pearl onions, herbs and garlic, resting on a bed of noodles, looked and smelled exceptional.

"I don't know yet," Thorn answered, when he'd had a taste of *coq au vin*. "I won't know that until I've had a look myself."

"About your parents—"

"And my brother. Don't forget him."

"They were killed in Colorado, weren't they?"

"Part of Kansas at the time."

"Which lies about twelve hundred miles from here, with two great mountain ranges in between, not mentioning the desert. Why would you expect to find your answers at Yreka."

"I have nothing in the way of expectations. Frankly, knowing what I do about your problem, a connection seems unlikely."

"Yet..."

"I need to know. And *you* should know three things. First, having me along will cost you nothing. Second, if it comes to fighting, I can be of help to you. And third, if you refuse me, I'll be following you anyway."

Conklin considered that, downing another bite of beef, and finally replied, "As to your first two points, I'm satisfied. This morning proved your nerve, beyond doubt. As to joining with the expedition, I'm afraid the final judgment must remain with those already signed on for the hunt."

"And they are...?"

"A diverse and motley crew," Conklin replied. "You'll meet some of them at the railroad depot, in the morning. The remainder will be waiting for us in Yreka. We shall put it to a vote. For what it's worth, mine falls to you."

"Suits me," Thorn said, determined to proceed as he had said, in any case. Before he stabbed another bit of *coq au vin,* he smiled and said, "This makes my first time hunting monsters in the mountains. I've already tried the desert and the plains."

THREE

APRIL 19, 1876

Thorn's train was leaving Sacramento's Central Pacific Railroad depot at 8:30 a.m., embarking on the ten-hour, 275-mile journey northward to Yreka, the seat of Siskiyou County. In preparation for the trip, he rose at half-past five o'clock, his gear already packed the night before, and shaved with cold water before he got dressed for the ride. Shadow and Bell, as Conklin had explained, would ride inside a special stock car with some of the expedition's other animals, cared for by a hostler Conklin had described as young but competent.

Thorn reckoned he would judge that for himself.

When he was dressed and fully armed, long guns aside, Thorn went down to the hotel's restaurant and ordered a heroic breakfast: scrambled eggs with bacon, ham, *and* sausage, jellied toast and strong black coffee on the side. Few other tenants of the Sacramento Arms were up and moving at that hour, but he nodded to a couple who reminded him of snake-oil salesmen, getting ready for another day of pounding doors or peddling wares on street-corners.

When he was done, paid up, and made a visit to the hotel's indoor lavatory, Thorn retrieved his saddlebags and his two rifles from his room upstairs. One was a Winchester repeater, the Model 1873, its fifteen-round magazine loaded with the same .44-40 rounds that fed his matching Colts. The other was a long-range piece, an 1872 Model Sharps chambered in .59-90 caliber, mounting a custom-made telescopic sight nearly the same length as its thirty-four-inch barrel, capable of scoring lethal hits beyond five hundred yards.

Eyes followed Thorn along the sidewalk as he walked down to the livery, his saddlebags across once shoulder and a rifle tucked beneath each arm to keep the guns from scratching one another. He imagined how he must look to the city's merchants, office workers, and the rest.

It almost made him smile.

His animals were ready, waiting for him, as he had requested prior to dining out with Conklin Tuesday night. However that meeting resolved itself, he'd planned on leaving for Yreka in the morning, had his railroad passage booked and paid for in advance. Approval from the lumber magnate was a bonus, but Thorn would have gone ahead without it as he'd promised Conklin, just the same.

The stallion and the mule both nodded in reply to Thorn's mute greeting, standing steady under their respective loads. Shadow was saddled, Bell bearing her pack of camping gear, though both would be unburdened for the long ride north, after Thorn had seen them safely settled in the stock car with their feed and water. As it was, he rode Shadow and led Bell to the railroad depot, picking out Reginald Conklin with three other men from his high seat, before he reached the platform and dismounted.

"Ah, good morning, Mr. Thorn," said Conklin, as he led the other three in their approach.

"Please make it Gideon."

"Agreed. And may I introduce three of our fellow travelers?" Without waiting for Thorn's response, he started in, naming his trio of companions left-to-right, while Thorn shook each man's hand in turn.

First up was Abel Durst, a functionary from the U.S. Department of the Interior, based in Sacramento but receiving orders from a boss in Washington, D.C. He was a slender man, around five-nine, red-faced as if from too much sun or alcohol, but he was sober now and didn't have a whiskey smell about him, in his checkered suit. His grip was dry but tentative, as if he wasn't ready to commit on short acquaintance.

Number two was Dr. Theo Minninger, the anthropologist from the Smithsonian back east. He studied bones but couldn't set a broken one, a task reserved, as Conklin had explained, for an expedition medic waiting in Yreka. Minninger had worn a three-piece suit, dark gray, and topped it with a bowler hat. A think moustache concealed his upper lip.

The third man was Jake Shandy, plump and jovial, identified as a reporter from the *San Francisco Chronicle*. "A snoop, that's me," he said, while pumping Thorn's hand with enthusiasm. "Anything that happens on this crazy trip, I write it down for publication." With a sidelong glance at Conklin, Shandy added, "No restrictions, guaranteed."

"Of course," Conklin agreed. "We have no secrets here. We'll either come back empty-handed, as our critics think, or else we'll bring home a surprise that will amaze the world. Whichever way it goes, we're trying what no man has done before. Now that we're all acquainted, shall we board?"

The train left right on time, sounding its whistle just in case some tardy traveler had missed the multiple conductors' calls for boarding and was sprinting madly to catch up. It started slowly, huffing clouds of steam that instantly put Thorn in mind of dragons, something that he definitely did not want to think about for ten long hours on the rails.

Been there, killed that, he thought, and tried to put the images of giant, hungry reptiles out of mind.

He sat apart from Conklin and the other three, not shunning them, but granting them sufficient privacy to carry on a conversation that, he guessed, they had begun some time ago. From louder snatches that he overheard, both Minninger and Durst had reservations about Conklin's expedition, although they were part of it. The anthropologist seemed adamant that they would fail, because the creature they were seeking was "impossible," devoid of any fossil record or other substantial evidence. He viewed the journey as a waste of time, but had his orders and was traveling on Conklin's dime in any case.

Durst, speaking for the government, had different concerns about the exercise. He understood the Yuroks had become "a problem" for white loggers working over their ancestral lands, but didn't like to see their legends given any credence by a group of white men who should know better. He mentioned military intervention, if the tribesmen were obstructing commerce, and that got an angry rise from Conklin, laying down in no uncertain terms his opposition to the use of soldiers in the great north woods.

Jake Shandy, for his part, abstained from interrupting unless questions came to mind, recording what he heard from Conklin and the others in a dog-eared notebook. When Conklin, Durst and Minninger went to the dining car, Thorn was about to follow, stomach growling now, but Shandy beat him to it, scurrying along the aisle, dropping into the plush seat facing Thorn's.

"Mind if I ask you a few questions?" he inquired.

"And if I did?"

"I'd slink away and try to find the answers somewhere else."

"Five minutes," Thorn replied, his stomach warning him of noon's approach.

"You seem to be the odd man out in this show," Shandy said. "You obviously know Conklin a little, but you only met the others at the depot and you sit apart from them. Why's that, I ask myself. All headed to the same place, for the same reason, and yet you seem to stand...let's say apart."

"Call me a late addition to the expedition's roster."

"Right. But it's been in the planning stage for well over two weeks. What brings you in at the eleventh hour, so to speak?"

"A combination of my curiosity and pure coincidence," Thorn said.

"Can you explain that for my readers?"

"Would they care?"

"When I tell them something's of interest, they care," Shandy replied, a trifle arrogant, full of himself.

"As to the curiosity, I read about the expedition and was suitably intrigued."

"And the coincidence?" Shandy was scribbling shorthand while he spoke, not looking at the notebook's page.

"I had the great good fortune to encounter Mr. Conklin yesterday, by accident, not far from my hotel. I did him a small favor, introduced myself, and here I am."

"When you say 'favor'..."

"If he wants to talk about it, Mr. Conklin can supply you with the details."

"Not a simple pay-off, then?" asked Shandy, smiling broader now as if to blunt what most would call a crass, offensive question.

Thorn smiled back at him, saying, "I'm not aware that Mr. Conklin needs my money. Now, if you'll excuse me..."

Thorn was on his feet and in the aisle when Shandy said, "Just one more question for the moment, please."

"What is it?"

"You've signed on to help Reg Conklin hunt for monsters that most people think are mythical, a bit of claptrap. What inspires a young man like yourself to spend his time this way?"

Thorn smiled and answered back, "Because I'm old enough to know most people can be wrong."

SISKIYOU COUNTY

"White men are coming," said the Yurok shaman called Ohanzee. That meant "shadow" in his people's language, and Ohanzee lived up to it with his reputation for predictive visions drawn from his multiple spirit guides.

"Soldiers?" Apisi asked. His tribal name, Coyote, fairly matched his face and wiry form.

"Not yet," Ohanzee said. "Later, perhaps, if these find what they seek."

"*Omah,*" Askook, the warrior named for serpents whispered, as if fearing to invoke the mountain devil if his voice carried beyond their *tipi*.

"Some of them crave knowledge only," Ohanzee replied. "Others would profit from whatever they may find—or else destroy it, out of fear and spite."

"No white man can destroy *Omah,*" Apisi said with perfect confidence.

"We do not know the limits of their medicine," Ohanzee said. "They fear being repelled from stolen lands. Their greed is powerful, their hatred more so."

"Hatred for our people?" Snake inquired.

"For anything in nature that opposes or impedes them," said the shaman. "They are strangers to the Great Spirit, claiming their so-called rights to anything they can, destroying what they cannot have."

"*We* can destroy *them,*" said Coyote. "They are strangers to the forest, unprepared for what awaits them there."

"To kill them brings the soldiers," said Ohanzee.

Plucking up his nerve, Snake challenged, "And they come regardless, do they not? If they find *Omah,* everyone will wish to see it, from the Great White Father to the lowest peasant."

"They will find what *Omah* lets them see," Ohanzee said. "But if they're killed—"

"Perhaps they only disappear," Coyote said. "People get lost forever in the big woods all the time, even a few of ours."

"Not lost," Ohanzee countered. "Some die naturally and are never found. Others may be devoured or transformed."

"Transformed?" There was a nervous sound to Askook's voice.

"Shape-shifters," said Apisi, trying to sound knowledgeable.

"No," Ohanzee said. "Shape-shifters, skinwalkers, change back and forth at will, or under a compulsion from the moon. A man transformed by *Omah* is forever lost to humankind."

"And what does he become, Old Father?" Apisi inquired.

"Whatever *Omah* shall decree for him."

"To keep that form forever?"

"Until death. A man transformed by *Omah* does not share in *Omah*'s immortality."

"How do we know they are immortal?" asked Coyote.

"From the wisdom of our ancestors, also because none has been found in death since first our people settled in this forest, many hundred winters gone."

"That simply means they were not found, Old Father," said Coyote. "I have never found a dead bear in the forest that I did not kill myself."

"You blaspheme!" said Ohanzee, scolding him. "The spirits hear your words and turn away their faces."

"No! Forgive me!"

"That is not for me to say, but I must reconsider your involvement in this thing."

Coyote almost cringed at that. "You know my dedication, Old Father. To our tribe and to *Omah,* who fights for us."

"You must remember that yourself," Ohanzee said. "That dedication is your own responsibility. I merely judge what I am shown."

"Believe in me, then," said Apisi, "for my heart is true."

"And you will follow orders? Do as you are told?"

"I will."

"The path before us will be difficult. Some of us may not see its end. Whatever sacrifice we make is preordained. The spirits call us now, and we can only answer with obedience."

Both warriors ducked their heads as one and muttered vows of fealty. Ohanzee smiled upon them as they met his eyes once more, his face crinkled like ancient buckskin, worn until it fairly shines.

"Tonight they come," he said. "It will be too late to begin their hunt. We follow in the morning, unobserved, and watch them closely."

"What if they find *Omah,* Old Father?" Coyote asked.

"I shall consult the spirits in that case and follow their directions, as shall you."

YREKA, CALIFORNIA

The town was nothing much to look at. Thorn's research had told him that it started as a mining camp, a quarter-century before, but unlike certain others had survived to prosper in its way, selected as the county seat for Siskiyou because the region's other settlements were even smaller, more remote. Yreka lay within the Shasta Valley, some forty miles north of a dormant volcano for which the valley was named. Mount Shasta—or North Mountain, in the local native tongue—loomed some eleven thousand feet above Yreka, with the dark bulk of the Siskiyous beyond it, marching northward as the night came on.

The train pulled it at seven o'clock, with dusk's shadows long in the streets around small shops and offices, a medium-sized hotel, a schoolhouse, church, and all the other trappings of a town that meant to stay and thrive. The only difference Thorn saw between Yreka and the other small towns he had visited across the West was its location, twenty-five hundred feet above sea level and hemmed in by dark, brooding forest.

After he disembarked, he saw to Bell and Shadow first, helping their keeper briefly burden them before Thorn led them down a steep ramp from the stock car to a street that had been plotted out but never paved. He got directions to the livery and led them there before the expedition's other horses were unloaded, while the four men he had traveled with were sorting out their bags. He found the stable dry and reasonably warm, considering the altitude and season, leaving them with thoughts of food and sleep, in care of a roly-poly hostler whose quick smile revealed a pair of gold incisors front and center.

Rooms were not a problem, Thorn already knew. Conklin had booked ahead at the hotel, and while he hadn't been expecting Thorn to tag along, he'd telegraphed to order up a spare after they had their conversation at *L'rotissarie français*. When logging money talked, it seemed that people in Yreka did their best to please.

At least, so far.

He still had hostile Yuroks to consider, claims of monsters in the woods, and any other undisclosed problems that might be playing hob with Conklin's company and personnel.

Thorn stashed his gear and long guns in the room allotted to him and was back downstairs for dinner with his future traveling companions as the clock struck eight. Their number had increased by three. The expedition's doctor, Caleb Heaton, was a man around Thorn's age, mid-twenties, trying mightily to grow a beard without too much success so far. The real surprise was Percy Manion and his aide, Ham Stotler, introduced to Thorn as trappers for the famous showman P. T. Barnum.

Shaking hands with Manion, Thorn asked, "Planning to catch *Omah* alive, are you?"

The husky redhead's mustache bristled as he answered. "Oh, alive or dead is all the same to me. The rubes will pay to see it, either way, although I grant you living's better. All that roaring through the bars and rattling its cage."

"And how would you propose to do that?" Thorn inquired.

"I always come prepared, son," Manion answered with a twinkle in his eye. "Don't fret yourself on that score."

Dinner was served collectively, no menu ordering. A staff of waiters brought their table fresh bread, heaping bowls of beans and mashed potatoes, gravy, salad, and a choice of platters bearing steaks and pork chops. Thorn ate heartily, hungry despite his visit to the railroad's dining car in transit, and said little while the others talked about their aspirations for the hunt.

Conklin's concern was getting matters back to normal at his logging camp, eliminating any further obstacles, while Abel Durst expressed concern for peaceful dealings with the Yurok tribe. Dr. Minninger assured them of his faith that they'd find nothing new or strange during their journey, indicating that he blamed hostiles or rogue bears for the deaths at Conklin's logging camp. The hunter, Manion, reassured them that his gear could handle anything they found, from killer bears to elephants, while Dr. Heaton voiced the hope that all of them would make it home intact. Jake Shandy interjected questions when he could and scribbled in his now-familiar notebook, eating less than anybody else while he was grabbing pithy quotes out of the air.

When the conversation turned to Thorn, he sketched his interest in mysteries without referring to his family and thanked Conklin again for welcoming him to the expedition. That got Conklin talking about yesterday's encounter with the toughs in Sacramento, and a few of those around the table—Manion, Stotler, and the newsman in particular—regarded him with something like a new respect. Or maybe that was only caution in their attitude, examining the wild card in their midst.

Thorn was relieved when they broke up and went off to their rooms for sleep, already looking forward to the morrow and whatever it might bring. He hoped there'd be no further killing, but whatever happened, he had come prepared.

FOUR

APRIL 20, 1876

Hotel waiters served the expedition's breakfast as they had dinner, the night before, with heaping plates of fried eggs and potatoes; bacon, ham, and sausage; thick toast and pancakes, with plenty of butter and syrup within easy reach. Hot coffee swept away the night's cobwebs and any trace of wayward dreams.

For Thorn's part, he was pleased at sleeping through the night without any disturbance. He had read somewhere that people always dreamed, without exception, but whatever memories or fantasies had crossed his mind in sleep were gone when he had squared himself away for traveling.

His outfit was the same as any other day, all black from head to toe except his white shirt underneath a vest and black string tie, but Thorm made a concession to the altitude and weather with addition of a thigh-length sheepskin coat. He tried it in his hotel room, ensuring he could reach his pistols and the Bowie knife without undue encumbrance, and was satisfied. A black wool scarf would keep the early chill of mountain spring from nipping at his neck, and if it rained...well, they would all get wet.

Thorn ate his share and then some before visiting the livery, where Bell and Shadow waited for him, growing slightly antsy in their stalls. He'd given them a fair idea of what was coming, based upon his own limited understanding of the hunt, and both were ready to set off, though Bell preserved her normal air of retisence that seemed unique to mules and goats.

Thursday was slated as an easy travel day, between Yreka and the logging camp where Conklin's three men had been killed. Work was suspended there, the loggers stopping short of calling it a strike, but holding out for action from the company to keep them safe around the clock. They were accustomed to the kind of timber-cutting accidents that left men dead or crippled, sometimes mutilated, but apparently the frights they had experienced of late were something else entirely, far beyond the incidental bloodshed they accepted calmly, almost with complacency.

So, no attacks between Yreka and the camp, if Conklin's estimation was correct. But just in case, Thorn had already double-checked his guns and felt he was prepared for anything that came his way.

Anything *normal,* that would be. As for the rest—what he'd come looking for, in fact—all bets were off.

As to the purported creature that they sought, *Omah,* Thorn still had no idea if it was purely legendary or if some of it, at least, was based in fact. *Something* had slaughtered three of Conklin's loggers, but Thorn hadn't seen the bodies and refused to speculate without more evidence as to responsibility. The killings raised grim memories of his departed family, but Conklin had been right in one respect: his private tragedy had happened more than twenty years and twelve hundred miles from the bloodshed in Siskiyou County.

Thorn preferred to think the present expedition would reveal a normal explanation for the violence, a relatively simple case of bear-eats-man, or even racial animosity at work. But he had also seen his share of strange events defying what most men regarded as natural law: a ghost town with actual ghosts in Kansas, seven months before, and prior to that, a real-life flying dragon down in Texas. Neither one fit into any scientific scheme of things he recognized from studies in the halls of academia, and there were times, awake or sleeping, when they haunted him.

Thorn shook it off and mounted Shadow, leading Bell through busy morning streets to join his traveling companions at the point they'd picked to rally for departure from Yreka. Townsfolk watched him pass with curious expressions on their faces, many of them certainly aware of what had happened at the logging camp and how Reginald Conklin hoped to settle it. As always, when he started on another quest, Thorn wondered whether he'd be passing through that way again, or if the strangers watching him were seeing him for the last time.

And if he died this time, would he find any answers waiting on the Other Side? *Was* there, in fact, another side to life, or was death simply the extinguishment of consciousness forever? His recent experience in Lazarus, the Kansas ghosttown, argued against death being a black, abysmal void—but did he really want to sample dwelling in the afterlife? And was there any choice?

Frowning at the morning now, Thorn rode on past the shops and offices to meet his team.

Ohanzee, flanked by his two warriors, saw the train arrive and watched the white men disembark. He knew the logging man, Conklin, by sight, and memorized the other faces from his expedition as they grouped around him, talking on the depot's platform. One of them—a strange man, marked in some way that Ohanzee did not understand as yet—soon left the others and retrieved two animals, a horse and mule, from the stock car appended to the train. He left the others at the depot, moving toward the stable where his beasts would spend the night.

"They are not many," Ascook said. "And they are soft."

"Not all of them," Ohanzee countered.

"We can kill them easily," Apisi opined. "Wait until they're in the forest and—"

"I give the word, not you," Ohanzee cut him off. "To strike is my decision, made in my own time, with consultation from the spirits."

"Yes, Old Father, but—"

"If you are not prepared to wait and follow orders," said the shaman, "then you are unwelcome on this quest."

"I hear and I obey," Coyote said.

"And I, Old Father," Snake echoed.

"Then we speak no more of killing until *I* say it is time. Before that happens, we trust *Omah* and the other spirits to defend their realm without assistance from a group of lowly men."

They stood concealed by sunset shadows in an alleyway between Yreka's railroad depot and a bar called the Last Chance Saloon. Concealment was not strictly necessary, as the peaceful Yurok often came to town for commerce, traveling in small groups, but Ohanzee saw no reason to announce his presence while the white hunters were getting organized. He doubted whether any of them knew his face—all natives looked the same to white eyes, as he'd heard it said—but why take chances?

Stealth was one of his best weapons as he aged, no longer young and strong in battle with his people's enemies. Stealth, and a connection to the spirits that few of his fellow Yuroks could achieve these days, with whites and their infernal engines of "advancement" pressing close on every side. Ohanzee trusted the Great Spirit and His minions, still able to wage war with invaders on their own behalf, however humble and debased the First Men had become.

Above all else, Ohanzee trusted *Omah,* angel of destruction chosen to defend Yurok ancestral lands.

The shaman had already done his part in summoning *Omah* to physical existence in the waking world. He could not take full credit—much of that belong to his opponents and their crass despoilment of the sacred land for money—but without the rituals he had performed, would *Omah* have appeared to battle in the flesh with the invaders? Truth be told, and while Ohanzee sought no glory for himself, he did not think so.

Battle had been joined already, at the logging camp. Three whites were dead, the others virtually paralyzed by fear of what they did not understand. That was a victory of sorts, but transitory. Only when the white men had been driven back from Yurok land decisively, forever, would the war be won.

The Yuroks who survived today lacked willpower, determination, and the strength to win that war themselves. They had begun to reckon they were "civilized." Ohanzee knew they needed an awakening, just as the white invaders needed to be taught that Old Gods still prevailed and would not idly watch while everything they had created was defiled by pallid worms.

"Come now," he told Snake and Coyote. "We have seen enough of them and know where they are going. They will first visit the logging camp, then travel on from there in search of *Omah*."

"Do we ride tonight?" Apisi asked.

"Don't worry," said Ohanzee, smiling. "I will not let you get lost."

Thorn met the other expedition members after checking into their hotel—aliteravely called Yreka's Rest—and spending a few moments in his third-floor room. When he returned downstairs and stepped into the hotel's restaurant, he spotted three new faces in the group and was in time to hear them introduced by Conklin.

"This is our support team, gentlemen," he said. "First up, Seamus O'Leary, our mule skinner handling transport of the gear and various essentials."

As he spoke, a stocky man with ginger muttonchops hiding a fair bit of his florid face stuck up a hand and nodded vaguely toward the others without asking or receiving any of their names.

"Next up, and some say most important on a trek like this," Conklin pressed on, "is Reno Lofton. He'll be cooking for us in the field."

The cook was bearded, somewhere in his fifties, with a weathered face and wiry build under his plaid shirt, black suspenders, and blue jeans tucked into knee-high boots. "I'm no gourmet," he told them, with a gap-toothed smile, "but I won't poison ya, neither."

Some members of the expedition laughed politely at his joke, eyes turning toward the odd man out. He was an Indian in buckskin, with a modicum of beadwork on the shirt, long hair pulled back and tied off in a ponytail behind.

"And this," said Conklin winding up his introductions, "is Migisi. He's a Yurok and will be our guide once we set off beyond the camp." Half-turning toward the guide, Conklin went on: "His name, I think, means 'Eagle'?"

The stoic tribesman nodded, offered no words in reply, his dark eyes scanning one white face after another. Thorn wondered whether he was sizing up the enemy or simply reading clients' faces before settiing off with them into the wilderness.

"Migisi won't be joining us for dinner, I'm afraid," Conklin advised. "Some rule the hotel has. But he'll be with us from tomorrow and beyond until our work is done." Conklin reached out to shake the Yurok's hand, a gesture that seemed awkward and pretentious with Migisi being exiled from the restaurant, but if it galled their guide, he didn't let it show. Thorn wondered how often since childhood he, Migisi, had been slighted and insulted in a host of ways dimwitted whites passed off as inoffensive.

When the Yurok had departed, they sat down with Conklin at their table's head, Thorn distant from him on the left. It was communal dining once again, this time with waitresses delivering the bowls and platters filled with beefsteak, ham, potatoes, carrots, fried mushrooms, gravy, and fresh-baked bread. Their coffee mugs were filled, and members of the team dug in, some talking with their mouths full of tomorrow's trek to reach the logging camp. Thorn listened, gleaning information from their chatter, while a part of his mind wondered where Migisi planned to spend the night, what he would eat, and how he felt about his role as guide for people who disdained him.

"I, for one, expect nothing," said Dr. Minninger, the anthropologist from Washington. "If such a thing as this *Omah* exists, where are the fossils? Why has no one bagged a specimen before, or simply found it dead beside a stream somewhere? Why is it only recognized today?"

Manion, the hunter, answered him. "First off, Doctor, there's nothing new about *Omah*. From Yurok tribesmen to the first white settlers, there have been tales of giant creatures in the woods throughout the great Northwest."

"All superstitious poppycock," said Minninger.

"You say that, coming from your office in the East," Manion replied. "But if you'd spolen to the elders as I have, you'd understand that they *believe* in this as strongly as you may believe in...well...in Jesus Christ himself."

The anthropologist bristled at that. "Surely," "you can't compare one with the other?"

"Only the degree of gullibility required for blind faith in a thing or person without substance," Manion answered.

"Sir—"

Conklin cut throguh the arument by tapping on his plate's edge with a butter knife. When he had everyone's attention, he declared, "We'll all have ample time to argue theories and beliefs around a campfire, on the trail. Tonight, let's celebrate the outset of an expedition that may either change the way we see our world, or else leave me remembered as a goddamned fool."

Laughter exploded, drowning any further arguments, and soon the simple task of chowing down preoccupied them all.

Reginald Conklin's eyes met Thorn's at the far end of the dining table, while around them, other members of the team discussed the weather and geography, techniques for big-game trapping, even the logistics of feeding a ten-man party in rugged terrain. The land they'd be traversing ruled out following the party with a normal chuck wagon, but they'd be working from the camp to start, and Reno Lofton told them he'd arranged to load ten days' worth of food and cooking utensils on pack mules, if they ranged farther afield. Seamus O'Leary, for his part, assured them that he'd keep the animals in line throughout their journey, come what may.

That said, the skinner turned to Thorn and said, "I understand you brought your own mule with you. We can add it to the train, and—"

"No thanks," Thorn replied, before O'Leary had a chance to finish.

"What say?" asked the Irishman, a tinge of added color rising in his ruddy cheeks,behind the muttonchops.

"I get along all right with Bell," Thorn said. "She'll stay with me."

"You named a mule?" O'Leary asked him, almost chel-lenging.

"Why not?"

O'Leary smirked at that and said, "I never knew a fellow fool enough to name a *mule*."

Instead of rising to the bait, Thorn said, "I guess your education's limited. You need to get out more."

"Is that right?" Seamus clutched his knife and fork in big, white-knuckled fists. "Mebbe you oughta educate me, then?"

"I'll try it, if you like," Thorn said, still smiling. "But I warn you that I haven't got much paitence for a futile exercise."

"A what?" O'Leary didn't seem to know if he should take offense or not.

Conklin cut in, saying, "I haven't introduced you all to Mr. Thorn, for which I must apologize. He's joining us at the last minute, after helping me resolve a problem back in Sacramento."

"Problem?" Dr. Minninger inquired, holding a piece of steak poised on his fork. "What sort of problem, may I ask?"

"It's all a bit embarrassing," Conklin confessed. "Yesterday morning, walking to the office, I was waylaid by a trio of armed men who clearly planned to rob me in broad daylight. Mr. Thorn was passing by and managed to discourage them."

"Discourage?" That from Percy Manion.

"He persuaded them that it would be a grave mistake if they laid hands on me, for which I owe him thanks."

"Persuaded, eh?" Manion eyed Thorn with new respect. "And what's your interest in this *Omah* business, Mr. Thorn?"

A tad reluctantly, Thorn said, "It's what I do. Investigating mysteries, that is. If I can celar them up, so much the better."

"Mysteries?" said Abel Durst. "What sort of mysteries?"

"All kinds," said Thorn. "As long as there's a decent riddle to it, I'm intrigued."

"Gideon Thorn!" Jake Shandy blurted out. "I *knew* I recognized the name. You stopped those cannibals back in Missouri, six or seven months ago. A family, I want to say they were. Named Lincoln? Landers?"

"Lindsay," Thorn replied. And then added, "Somebody had to do it."

"But the sheriff hadn't managed, all those years," Shandy observed. "I wondered whether there was more to that than met the eye, or wound up on the printed page."

"Sometimes the locals get too close to something," Thorn suggested. "They can't see the forest for the trees."

"Well," Conklin interrupted, "there'll be plenty trees where we're going. They question now is whether something's hiding in amongst them, killing loggers when they go about their jobs."

Dr. Minninger regarded Conklin with an eyebrow raised. "You don't believe this monster nonsense, do you, Mr. Conklin?"

"No sir," Conklin said. "I don't believe in anything. Belief implies blind faith in things that can't be seen or understood. I *know* that someone or some*thing* butchered three of my men. Whoever or whatever is responsible, I have a score to settle there. A business and employees to protect. I mean to pay that bill in full, regardless of the cost, and make damned sure that nothing like it ever reoccurs."

A couple of the expedition members clapped when he was done, most of them peering down the table's length at Conklin or returning to their food before it cooled too much. Thorn's eyes, the farthest from him, studied Conklin with frank curiosity before they turned back toward the young man's plate.

FIVE

APRIL 20, 1876

Expedition members gathered in the restaurant at the Yreka's Rest a short half-hour after sunrise, Thursday morning, seeming more subdued than they had been the night before. Some, Thorn supposed, had sat up late debating what they hoped to find, if anything, while age and deviation from their standard hours in an office might be catching up with others, most specifically the anthropologist from Washington. He wasn't old, per se, but he had spent his working life in dusty alcoves, sorting bones with no greath sense of urgency.

The liveliest among them, after Thorn himself, were Percy Manion and the stockman, Seamus O'Leary. Thorn supposed the hunter must be looking forward to a great adventure—and the fee he would collect from P. T. Barnum if he managed to retrieve a specimen.

Thorn knew Barnum by reputation, though they'd never met and he had not attended any of the showman's famous exhibitions. What he knew, from small talk, was that Barnum seemed to pride himself on tricking yokels with illusions like the "Feejee mermaid," stitched together from the dessicated carcasses of fish and monkey to astound the credulous, or by exploiting malformed humans in his freak shows. Rumor credited Barnum with saying "Nobody ever lost a dollar by underestimating the taste of the American public" and "There's a sucker born every minute," though Barnum himself denied both rude remarks. Barnum *had* offered fifty thousand dollars for the carcass of a monster said to swim about in Lake Champlain, never collected, and it stood to reason that he'd match that figure if an *Omah* fell into his greedy hands, alive or dead.

While Manion joshed with his assistant, Stotler, and had less success with a subdued Reginald Conklin, Thorn tucked into breakfast: fried eggs and potatoes, griddle cakes, and beans, ignored by most around the table until Seamus O'Leary called to him from midway down and caught him with his mouth full.

"Change your mind about me handling that mule of yours?" O'Leary asked.

"No, thanks."

O'Leary frowned and shook his head, as if he had received sad news about an ailing relative. "Afraid you'll have to trail the pack, then," he declared. "Can't have a stranger with an unsecured animal hold up the train I've organized."

It felt like he was looking for an argument, but Thorn defused it for the moment. "Suits me fine," he said. "I don't mind bringing up the rear."

O'Leary blinked at him, as if he'd answered in a foreign tongue, then shrugged him off and bent back to his loaded plate. With any luck, Thorn hoped, the Irishman would let it go at that and they could stay out of each other's way for the remainder of the expedition. Otherwise, if he tried anything with Bell or Shadow, Thorn would have to set him straight in no uncertain terms.

After breakfast and protracted visits to the hotel's privy, members of the team gathered around Yreka's stable, where O'Leary's mules had spent the night with horses delegated to the trackers. Some of the participants were clearly novices at riding horseback, grumbling as they took time mounting up and managing the reins. O'Leary told them that he'd chosen horses for their stamina and even temperaments, but that appeared to carry little weight with Dr. Minninger or Abel Durst. Their team physician, on the other hand, swung up into his saddle like a seasoned hand, with Conklin and the others managing all right.

Migisi had rejoined them after breakfast, mounted bareback on a tobiano pony that seemed built in equal parts for speed and long days on the trail. He wore the same buckskins and had a Henry rifle slung across his back, secured with a length of rope he'd tied around the muzzle and the stock. His only other weapon was a long knife on his belt, secured in a fringed and beaded sheath.

Conklin had no words for the team as they set out, Thorn parked on Shadow at the tail of Seamus O'Leary's six-mule team. He simply scanned the line of faces watching him, then nodded to Migisi in the lead, and they began their journey northward to the logging camp.

When they were half an hour from Yreka, Percy Manion nudged his brindle gelding closer to the rubicano mare his sidekick rode. Ham Stotler raised a bushy eyebrow, silent question posed.

"If we get lucky," Manion said, "remember that we get more for this *Omah* thing alive, if possible. Boss likes 'em rattling the cage bars, giving rubes the chills."

"I got it," Stotler said. "You really think there's anything to this?"

"Beats me," Manion replied, "but something killed those loggers, and with any luck, we'll get a close-up look at it."

"Nets might not hold it," Stotler said. "They're good for bear, but if this thing exists, from what they say, it makes a grizzly look like somebody's old hound dog."

"Then we've got the other," Manion said. "Dead or alive, but breathing gives us both a larger bonus."

"Yeah, I guess."

The "other" Manion spoke of was an express rifle made in London by Holland & Holland, a four-gauge with barrels mounted side by side in shotgun style. It fired bullets that weighed close to a quarter-pound apiece, ensuring death to anything that man had ever seen on the receiving end. Manion had used the gun on elephants, rhinoceros, and hippopotamus, with no complaint except the bruising to his shoulder from its sharp recoil. If *Omah* could withstand that lethal force, it was indeed a dweller of some other realm where scientific laws did not apply.

"I'm thinkin' about how we pack it out," Stotler announced, after a silent moment passed.

They'd talked about it, naturally, but the disassembled cage that two of Seamus O'Leary's mules were carrying seemed frail now, when he thought about it.

"We've already covered that," Manion replied.

"I know but—"

"But nothing. If it's alive, the cage will hold it. Built for anything up to a polar bear, you know, case-hardened steel on all the bars. We've got the dope, too, you'll remember."

Chloral hydrate that would be, which Manion figured he could put in meat or anything at all a forest-dwelling monster liked to eat. It would be dead weight after that, until the dose wore off, no difference than hauling out a carcass when you came right down to it, unless the damned thing woke up halfway back to camp.

And failing that, he had the four-gauge standing by, already loaded for the kill.

But bagging such a thing alive would be the pinnacle of his career—at least, until somebody found a living, breathing dinosaur just begging to be caught and caged. Meanwhile, Manion would settle for the cash and glory that came with delivering a real-life legend into P. T. Barnum's circus tent.

Omah stops in its tracks and sniffs the forest air. A change is coming, not of seasons, which it understands, but in the very atmosphere. More pallid creatures coming to disturb it, with their beasts of burden and their tools, reeking of black powder and oil.

Searching for *Omah* in the forest? Possibly.

Omah knows nothing of the varied names applied to it by mankind, be it *Skookum, Seatco, Bukwas, Nan'tina, Gilyuk, So'yoko, Iktomi,* or any of the others used by tribes that recognize its physical existence in the world they share. It neither knows nor cares that some revere it as a spirit of the wild, while others view it as a demon sent to punish them for some transgression they cannot recall. What use is any of their jabber-talk to one who never changes, only seeks to dwell in peace and undisturbed?

But now the man-things have disturbed *Omah*, invading its homeland with tools, wagons, and lesser animals, intent on leveling its forest like a swarm of locusts ravaging a farmer's crops. The darker people, those it is accustomed to from generations of exposure, hide away for the most part, singing and chanting uselessly, as if they hope Nature may intervene somehow to stem the tide.

But there is only *Omah* to forestall the ravagers.

It tried to frighten them at first, convince them that it was unhealthy to pursue their depredation. They were unconvinced and mounted guards against it, then dispatched a hunting party to the forest after nightfall—fools—hoping to find *Omah* and kill it. As if it were only one, and not a tribe unto itself, inhabiting the woodlands long before the first dark men appeared, trekking across the land bridge between continents, over a stormy, partly-frozen sea.

The first intruders had been almost meek, respectful of the land and its inhabitants, unlike the pale ones who claimed everything within their sight as theirs and theirs alone. As far as it could feel such things, *Omah* regretted their appearance on the scene and wished them gone, by any means available. If that meant war between their species, then so be it.

Let the war begin.

In fact, first blood had already been spilled. The foolish hunters who'd come seeking *Omah* after sundown were no more. Survivors from the logging settlement had carted off their pitiful remains, and what would happen next?

Omah expected escalation, though it did not recognize that word or any other spoken by its enemies. They were advancing even now, in greater numbers than before, intent on what they might describe as victory.

So be it.

Omah was prepared. The war would not be swift for its opponents, and if they should triumph in the end, there would be many fewer of them than had started out the fight.

Because *Omah* was not alone.

The logging camp was quiet when Reginald Conklin's expedition reached it, Thorn relaxed and happy on his stallion, bringing up the rear with Bell. Along the way, he'd tried to probe the looming forest with his mind, hoping for any kind of contact with an unexpected creature, but the whispers that came back to him were all from deer, raccoons and possums, rodents and the like. Reptiles were present but cared little for communication. Birds, or most of them, were too aloof to listen or respond.

A group of silent loggers, many bearing axes, picks and shovels as if they were weapons, met the group when it arrived, some glaring at Migisi riding point, then warming up at sight of Conklin and the other whites behind him. When they closed around their boss, aboard his leopard Appaloosa stallion, they began to babble greetings and expressions of a wish to be long gone.

"All of you settle down, please," Conklin said. "Nobody's going anywhere right now. You're under contract to the company, and leaving means the end of any money you have coming. But the *good* news is, we've come to put things right, and I'll be here beside you till it's done."

From Thorn's position, Conklin's promise failed to move most of the lumberjacks. They muttered bleak dissatisfaction but apparently could not afford to leave without the pay they'd earned so far, much less depart on foot without another job on the horizon. Conklin clearly sensed their mood, and mindful of the tools-turned-weapons many of them carried out to greet him, raised his voice again.

"We're too late to begin the hunt today," he told the upturned, angry faces. "You've already seen what happens when you try it in the dark. First thing tomorrow morning, we'll be up and at it, tracking down whatever hurt your friends and—"

"Killed, not hurt!" one of the loggers interrupted, shouting it.

"And I apologize for that. Of course, they lost their lives, and I'm investigating means to compensate their families, if any can be found. Now, as I said, first thing tomorrow we'll be out and hunting down whatever *killed* your friends, ensuring that the same thing won't happen again as work goes on."

"Who guards the camp while you're out hunting?" asked another lumberjack.

"Why, *you,* its residents," Conklin replied. "Who else? And to facilitate defense, we've brought six brand-new Winchester repeaters with us, to distribute on the basis of seniority. Whoever or whatever may come creeping around camp, that kind of firepower will lay them low."

More muttering, but some of them were also nodding now, if cautiously, at least partly persuaded by their boss's words. How long that acquiescence would survive, if there were more attacks, was anybody's guess.

"Now, if you'll let us pass," Conklin called out to his

employees, "we've brought you a special cook and beefsteak for the lot of you, to celebrate a turning of the tide."

Reluctantly, it seemed, the crowd of loggers passed and let them through, riding into the heart of camp, with Thorn drawing his share of dubious assessment at the party's rear.

"The white hunters are here," Ohanzee told his warriors. "Can you smell them?"

Askook and Apisi sniffed the breeze and frowned as one, exchanging glances. Askook grunted noncommittally. Apisi shrugged and said, "I smell *something,* Old Father."

Ohanzee scowled at them, thinking, *Young people. Where is their respect for the old ways?*

At least the two of them were fighters, tested in the field and proven strong. That trait would come in handy soon, even if neither one of them fully appreciated how the shaman's vision would transform the world they knew. Such youthful ignorance depressed Ohanzee, but he recognized that times had changed from when he was a boy, learning his craft from Yurok elders in a time when white men rarely troubled members of the tribe and posed no threat to their environment.

Now, whites were everywhere, consuming everything, and while they'd fought a bitter war amongst themselves to liberate the dark ones they held captive, it made matters worse than ever for the red men who were there so long before them. Now, the locust hordes were pushing westward by the tens or thousands, claiming land meant for the use of all by the Great Spirit, hemming it about with fences, cutting down the trees, and gouging up the soil for so-called precious metal. If no line was drawn, if they continued unopposed, the world they had supposedly discovered would be ravaged and picked clean, unfit for human life.

Ohanzee meant to draw that line and hold it fast, with *Omah*'s help. And to that end, he knew he must commune once more with beings greater than himself.

"I need to pray," he told Apisi and Askook. "Leave me."

The warriors did not question him, but simply rose and faded back into the shadowed woods. Ohanzee guessed they were relieved that he excluded them from prayers, which they would probably have garbled anyway. As children, they had doubtless heard their elders speaking, but Ohanzee sensed they had not *listened,* taking in the vital lessons that were offered to them free of charge. Such was the way of children in the modern age, expecting life to carry them along and never change.

But there were hard times coming, and Ohanzee knew he would be in the midst of them. He could not see how they might be resolved, or whether he'd survive the battle yet to come, but if he fell along the way, at least his place within the Ghost World was assured. He would have done his best and fought on to the end for the Great Spirit and the others he directed in defense of Mother Earth.

The hunters, as he knew, would be well armed and confident as only fools could be, when they began their quest. With three men dead so far, they wanted vengeance, like a mob tracking a common murderer with ropes and torches. They had no more comprehension of the power they confronted, of *Omah* itself, than children cast into the wilderness and told to find their way alone.

Ohanzee wished them all dead.

And if he should die defending that which he held dear, he would not be alone.

Such was the price each generation had to pay for preservation of itself, its offspring, and the land it held in trust for future generations. White men failed to grasp that concept, raped the very soil itself in search of transitory wealth, and would be judged accordingly.

Ohanzee knew that he was not their judge, only an instrument of the Great Spirit in the long war that the pale invaders brought upon themselves when they set foot in the "New World." That very concept in itself was blasphemous, as if mere mortals could discover nature's miracles, crafted eons before their ancestors first crawled from European caves and gaped in wonder at the sky above.

Their time was coming, but it would not be the victory they fantasized.

If *Omah* and Ohanzee had their way, the enemy would be cast down forever and would trouble Earth no more.

SIX

Supper in the camp's mess hall was not the celebration Conklin had envisioned. There was beefsteak, true enough, with all the trimmings thanks to Reno Lofton, but the loggers clearly were not in a mood to either sing their boss's praises or to buy his promises that all would soon be well. The foreman and a few others carried the new rifles that Conklin's pack train brought to camp, while others turned up with a motley collection of firearms and tools of their trade, as if preparing to defend the dining hall against attack.

Thorn, in the spirit of the evening, had worn his Colts and Bowie knife as usual. He didn't know what might transpire from that point on, but whatever it was—if anything—he meant to be prepared.

He sat with Conklin, other members of the hunting party, and camp foreman Ed Russell at one of the dining hall's four long tables, listening for comments from the lumberjacks, surprised that they were mostly silent while they ate. In other circumstances, he'd have banked on boisterous behavior, winding down another day of labor in the forest, but tonight, apparently penned up in camp for days, they shared a sullen mood of dark anticipation tinged with fear.

Thorn was positioned next to Russell at the table, two seats down from Conklin, facing Dr. Minninger across the rough-hewn planks. When all of them had focused on their plates a while, he turned and asked Russell, "I don't suppose it's possible to view the bodies of the men you lost?"

The foreman looked at him askance and asked, "What for?"

"We're hunting whatever it was that killed them," Thorn reminded him. "The wounds might help us work out what that was."

Russell suppressed a shudder as he said, "They weren't just kilt, Mister, but torn apart. I mean that like it sounds. And no, they can't be seen, unless you wanna dig 'em up from where we planted 'em. I doubt the other boys would take kindly to that."

"I understand," Thorn said. "But if you could describe the injuries..."

"I told you: torn apart. Not like a bear will gut a man and gnaw around the edges, or a wolf pack takes the soft bits first. I saw 'em fresh, and see 'em still, up here." An index finger tapped his skull. "It looked like something huge got hold of 'em and started rippin' pieces off the way a crazy child might tear a doll apart. O' course, some bits were *missin'* too, and there were bite marks on a couple of the bodies, like whatever kilt 'em took out time to feed."

Thorn pressed his luck. "And can you estimate the bite marks' size?"

Russell grimaced, set down his knife and fork, then raised his two big hands and held them six or seven inches from each other, fingers curled to make a kind of open circle. "Right around that size," he said, then let his hands drop to his lap.

"And not a bear, you say."

"I've seen men mauled by bears before, grizzly and black bears, both. They claw a man, as well as biting him, and there was none of that with our men. Biting, yes, but only on the meaty bits. The rest was more like twisting, pulling them apart, till things came outa joint or just ripped open."

Staring at the rare beef on his plate, Russell pushed it away.

"I'm sorry for the questions."

"Nah, forget it. I still see 'em every time I close my eyes."

Russell turned on the bench they shared, got up, and left the dining hall, his new repeating rifle tucked under one arm. Thorn watched him go, then turned back to his meal and finished it while those around him went on hashing out small details of the day to come, when they would finally begin their hunt.

Omah smells meat charring and wonders whey the small, pale creatures spoil their food with fire. It reinforces first impressions that the beings come to claim its forest are a weaker species, ignorant, even pathetic if they weren't so ravenous, despoiling everything they touch. The three already sent to track *Omah* were easy kills, despite the seeming weapons that they carried, ripe with smells of oil and metal. None had served to keep them safe, and *Omah* sees no reason to believe the next group, although larger, will be any different.

Because *Omah* is legion.

It has no name for its kinfolk in the forest, gathered to confront a challenge that affects them all. *Omah* is name enough, and even that is foreign to the creature's thoughts, applied by other men, the red ones. When *Omah* thinks of itself, its scattered tribe, names are irrelevant. It simply *is*, a force spawned by the woodlands, neither friend nor enemy to smaller species, unless it is hungry or the pale ones force its hand.

How many times has *Omah* seen them in the forest, passing through, hunters and trappers seeking game? If they move on, they hold no interest for *Omah,* no reason for it to challenge them. But when they come to stay and start to change the landscape, felling trees and driving other animals away, *Omah* discerns a need to intervene and stop the plunder.

While the red men sit around their lonely fires and chant its name in vain, *Omah* is on alert. It knows the forest's ways better than any man, of any color, and can move unseen through light and shadow like the spirit some mistake it for. Even in groups, *Omah* can travel almost silently, footsteps aside. When hunting, one or more of them can strike without warning, short bursts of speed equivalent to any deer's, their bulk and strength matching all but the largest bear's. *Omah*'s diet, including meat and plants alike, does not restrict its movements. It sleeps lightly, when the mood strikes, and can wake to sudden action in a heartbeat, clear of eye and mind.

The pale, small men are nothing by comparison, despite their weapons that can strike down smaller species from a distance, with a sound and smell of smoky thunder. None has ever slain *Omah,* or even grazed a member of its tribe. *Omah* believes they never will.

But even if it comes to that, a battle to the death of one tribe or the other, *Omah* has no fear. Its life goes on until it one day ends, usually without warning in advance. Such things are only natural, and till that day arrives, *Omah* stands ready to defend its home at any cost. The smaller creatures that oppose it do so at their peril, and may not survive to learn from their mistake.

After dinner and the usual good-nights to other members of the expedition, Thorn went off to find the privy—which turned out to be a slit trench dug some distance from the logging camp, downhill. When he was finished there, taking advantage of an old newspaper nailed to a tree trunk, he stopped to have a quiet word with Bell and Shadow, then proceeded to the tent that had been set aside for him.

The camp's loggers slept in bunkhouses, under roofs, surrounded by log walls, but Conklin's foreman had informed them on arrival that the bunks were full, except for three vacated by the recent dead, now treated by the rest as out of bounds, perhaps bad luck to touch them, much less climb under their blankets. Thus, the tents, except for Conklin, who would sleep inside the camp's office, behind a stout locked door.

The tents were one- and two-man models. Where it seemed appropriate, the occupants were paired up: Percy Manion with Ham Stotler; Dr. Minninger with Abel Durst; Seamus O'Leary with the expedition's cook, Lofton. The smaller one-man tents were set aside for Thorn, Jake Shandy. Dr. Heaton, and the expedition's guide, Migisi—whose canvas shelter had been situated farthest from the central fire, almost as if the loggers who erected it were hoping he might catch a chill.

Perhaps because he had been raised in equal parts by Aunt Drusilla and her African retainer, Gideon Thorn failed to grasp the racial animosity that caused such gaping fissures in American society from coast to coast. He understood that it existed and had seen its ill effects firsthand—from cruel gibes against minorities at Weatherford Academy to Harvard's restrictive quota for Jewish admissions, plus brawling conflict from the streets of Boston to the Wild West—but he missed the reason for it. Part of it, Thorn knew, was drawn from misinterpretation of religion, while the rest struck him as a mixture of fear and ignorance, stirred by envy conjured from the darker corners of some damaged minds.

Inside his pup tent, Thorn was pleased to find that none of his belongings were disturbed. He hadn't reckoned anyone would try to tamper with them, and it pleased him to be right, but still he checked his rifles to make sure that they were loaded and in working order, just in case.

Hoping to be prepared throughout the night to come, Thorn shed his coat, vest, tie and boots, but otherwise lay down completely dressed, his gunbelt coiled beside him with both pistols and his Bowie close at hand before he pulled one of his two allotted blankets over him. The other served Thorn as a ground cloth, since the tent possessed no floor, while some adjustment to his saddlebags sufficed for them to be his pillow.

More than halfway through the month of April, snow had finally departed from the northern California woods, but daytime temperatures still plummeted after the sun went down. Thorn didn't envy the selected loggers who'd been set as guards around the camp—nor, truly, after what he'd heard about the three men who were killed, was he convinced that men and guns would keep *Omah,* whatever it might be, from striking when and where it chose.

Memories of his family were inescapable as Thorn closed his eyes, hoping to sleep. Though ancient now, considering his age, how far he'd come in life, the images that he recalled from that night in his second year were still as clear as if they'd happened yesterday: a howling in the middle of a Rocky Mountain storm, a looming shape that crashed the doorway to his parents' cabin, and the carnage that ensued before young Gideon, miraculously, made his getaway with nothing but a gash across his scalp to show for it.

Dumb luck, or had there been some guiding hand at work?

As usual, that last, insoluble conundrum carried him away into the murky realm of sleep.

Jake Shandy huddled in the shadow of the camp's mess hall, crouching outside an open window with his notebook and a pencil in his hands. Inside, too far away for him to touch but close enough to eavesdrop on, Reginald Conklin lingered at a table with the circus hunter, Percy Manion, Dr. Minninger from Washington, and Abel Durst speaking for the Interior Department. Conklin and Manion had fenced lightly with the other two at supper, but after the lumberjacks and other members of their team cleared out, Shandy remaining close enough to hear and scribble shorthand notes, their conversation grew more serious.

"Sometimes," Conklin was saying now, "I wonder if the

pair of you weren't sent specifically to watch me fail, *hoping* the expedition fails."

Durst's voice came back, saying, "I can assure you, sir, that such is not the case, at least for me. My agency, of course, prefers that there be no disturbance in the *status quo,* as far as logging and the natives are concerned. A war would be unwelcome, possibly disastrous. As to this supposed creature that you seek...well, frankly, no one whom I've spoken to quite takes it seriously. And with Mr. Barnum thrown into the mix—"

"Be careful," Percy Manion cautioned him. "I'll have no slander spoken in regard to my employer. He's an honest businessman—"

"Who profits from the ignorance of hicks," Minninger interrupted. "As for the Smithsonian, we seriously doubt that any large primate will be discovered here, when they are clearly foreign to the continent—indeed, the hemisphere. The nearest relatives would be small monkeys found in South America, completely absent from the fossil everywhere above the Isthmus de Tehuantepec in southern Mexico."

"And if you're wrong, Doctor?" Manion inquired.

Minninger took a moment, cleared his throat, and said, "It would, or course, rewrite most of our scientific texts, with major implications for religious theory. We've seen how Darwin has already raised a tempest with *The Origin of Species,* followed by his latest, *The Descent of Man.* If someone should present a living specimen—"

"And there it is!" said Conklin. "Wishing failure on the expedition, so your precious dogmas from the ancient past won't be upset."

"Sir," Minninger replied stiffly, his voice taut, "as a

scientist I can assure you that I welcome any new discoveries with open arms. At the same time, however—"

Shandy heard a footstep close behind him, rose from where he'd crouched beside the open window with a smile already forming as he turned to find Seamus O'Leary peering at him. "Somethin' I can help you with?" the hostler asked.

Shandy thought fast, raising his notepad as he said, "I dropped this on the way back to my tent. Slit trench and all, I couldn't let it fall out of my pocket into all that—"

"Slippery, is it?" O'Leary cut him off, eyes shifting toward the open mess hall window close at hand.

The newsman answered with a quick, diversionary question of his own. "Are you expecting any problems on the journey, herding donkeys through the forest?"

"I herd *mules,*" the older man corrected him. "And they go where I tell 'em, or they feel the whip."

"No problems, then," Shandy replied, pretending to jot down a note. Flashing another grin, he said, "Until tomorrow, sir," and left O'Leary standing in the shadows as he angled toward his one-man tent beside the fire.

It was after midnight when the howls woke Thorn from vague dreams of a snowstorm in another time, another place. He sat up in the pup tent, wide awake within a heartbeat, twin Colt Peacemakers in hand and cocked before he realized the sounds were coming from a distance and posed no imminent threat.

After he eased the hammers down and slipped one pistol back into its holster, Thorn crawled to the tent flap, opened it, and stuck his head outside. The central fire was burning down but still shed light enough for Thorn to see the posted guards collected near the mess hall, heads bent as they joined in whispered consultation. Each was clinging to his Winchester repeater like a life preserver on a ship beset by stormy seas, heads swiveling to scan the darkened forest that surrounded them.

Not an illusion, then, and nothing conjured from his dreams.

Thorn left his tent and stood upright, feeling the midnight chill through his shirtsleeves and trousers, the right-hand pistol dangling beside his thigh. Some sleepy loggers were emerging from the bunkhouses, milling about and jabbering as the unnerving howls echoed from nowhere in the night.

After a moment, Thorn decided there were two sources for the unearthly cries, one somewhere east of camp, the other ululating from the north. He couldn't stretch his own imagination to describe it as communication, but the howls *did* seem to answer one another, as coyotes sometimes will when they are baying at the moon. After a lull, just when he thought the cries were winding down, there came a high-pitched chittering, somehow both shrill and throaty all at once, that instantly reminded Thorn of monkeys jabbering inside a circus cage.

When that cacophony subsided, finally, silence descended on the forest and the logging camp. By that time, every expedition member was awake and on his feet, along with forty-odd loggers and their employer. Conklin had pulled trousers on over long underwear before he left his quarters, carrying a rifle of his own, eyeing the darkness with a fierce expression on his face by firelight.

Once the noise had stopped, he shouted at his men, "All right! Show's over! I have no idea what that was all about, but it's the reason why we're here to help. The hunt begins tomorrow, first thing after breakfast, and we won't stop searching till we have an answer for your troubles. One way or another, I *will* solve this, and the work you all were hired for *will* proceed."

Thorn heard the loggers muttering at that, but none of them raised any protest to their boss. After a moment, when the whispers started dying down, Conklin advised then, "Back to sleep now, boys. Tomorrow is another early day, and help's at hand!"

Watching the company's vice president retreat into his cabin, Thorn wondered if it would be that simple, after all—and which of them would see it through until the end.

SEVEN

APRIL 21, 1876

Breakfast was steak and eggs, another bonus for the lumberjacks, although it didn't seem to lift their spirits after last night's eerie interruption of their sleep. Over their plates, they groused and grumbled, shooting glances at the expedition members which, if not exactly hostile, clearly showed a lack of confidence that any of their recent problems would be solved by their employer, eight white strangers, and a Yurok Indian.

At breakfast, Dr. Minninger expounded on his theory for what he referred to as the prior night's "entertainment." Knife and fork in hand, he told the other expedition members, "I suspect that all we heard were normal forest animals, well known to any scientist. The howling would, of course, be gray wolves or their smaller relatives, *Canis latrans*—that is, coyotes, to the layman."

"And the chattering that followed it?" Jake Shandy asked, notebook beside his plate and pencil at the ready.

"Why, nothing but raccoons, the common *Procyon*

lotor," said Minninger. "Most people do not realize the volume they can generate during a state of sexual excitement, or while fighting over scraps of food."

Across the table from him, Percy Manion laughed and said, "Raccoons? If you think those were 'coons, Doc, I believe you've spent too much time in a lab."

"I beg your pardon, sir, but—"

Conklin tapped his fork against his coffee mug, commanding their attention. "Gentlemen, we have no time for arguments this morning. Whatever the source of last night's sounds, three of my men were *not* killed and dismembered by raccoons or any other common forest denizen. We have a job to do this morning, and I urge you all to hurry up. I plan to leave in thirty minutes, with or without stragglers."

Thorn was nearly finished with his meal, and Conklin's order made the others hurry, gulping down their food and leaving plates for Reno Lofton to collect when they were gone. The party soon assembled near the ashes of the past night's bonfire, Thorn mounted on Shadow, while the rest rode horses Conklin had supplied. Bell would remain in camp, along with four mules from the train. Seamus O'Leary would be leading two behind the hunting party, as he told the others, just in case they stumbled onto something. Both were packing nets and other gear for Percy Manion and his aide, presumably hoping to catch *Omah* alive.

Thorn, for his part, was packing both his Winchester and long-range Sharps as they set out in single file, Migisi leading, trailed by Conklin and the rest. He didn't know if *Omah* physically existed, though the noises that he'd heard last night inclined him to suspect it. If the creature *was* a thing of flesh and blood, if there were several at large in fact, Thorn meant to have sufficient firepower on hand.

"You think we'll turn up anything?" Jake Shandy asked him, catching up to Gideon aboard his bay gelding.

Thorn shrugged and said, "You heard as much last night as I did. What do you think?"

"Undecided," Shandy said, "but hoping."

"That we find a monster?"

"Why not?" Shandy answered, beaming. "I can see the headlines now."

"And your name on the story," Thorn suggested.

"Hell, yes! I'm the only game in town on this one."

"Are you armed?" Thorn asked him.

"I'm prepared," Shandy replied, patting a pocket of the long duster he wore over his normal clothes.

"A pocket pistol?"

"Better," Shandy said. "A sawed-off Schofield .44. I lose some range with only half the barrel, but I'm not much of a marksman anyhow. Up close, it does just fine."

"Against a grizzly or a cougar?"

The newsman's answer was another careless smile. "The rest of you are packing guns enough to keep me safe," he said. "I'm here to write, not fight."

Thorn let it go, hoping the young man wasn't in for a surprise.

Ohanzee and his warriors trailed the hunting party at a distance, moving parallel along the white men's track and eastward of them, well beyond their line of sight. The shaman's main concern, that his trio might be detected by the Yurok traitor guiding the intruders, quickly passed when no alert was sounded from the column.

Ohanzee had glimpsed the Yurok guide but did not know him, though Askook identified him as Migisi, friendlier with white men than a tribesman ought to be, although the whites still treated him with thinly veiled contempt. That meant they did not spit on him or physically attack him—unless they were drunk, perhaps—but neither was Migisi treated as a full-fledged human being by the immigrants from Europe who now claimed what they still called "the New World" as their own.

Ohanzee had been pleased, nearly ecstatic, when his prayers evoked an audible response from *Omah* in the middle of the night. Those sounds would terrorize the loggers at their camp and give the hunters second thoughts about their search for something they would never fully understand. Their conquest of the continent to this point made them doubly arrogant, convinced that even Nature bowed before them in abject obeisance, but they were helpless in the face of powers unimagined by their tiny minds.

Askook and Apisi still craved combat with the hunters, nagging Ohanzee sporadically for his permission to attack—if not by daylight, then at nightfall, when the whites were tired and could not trace the source of arrows flying through the darkness. One or two kills at a time would satisfy them, while they waited for *Omah* to do its part, but still the shaman stood firm and refused them. He would recognize the moment when it came, if ever.

Omah needed no assistance from the likes of Coyote and Snake, as ardent as they were for contact with the common enemy.

The hunting party traveled slowly, even though its members all were mounted, some displaying more skill with their animals than others. Coming up behind, one of the whites led two pack mules. Ohanzee did not know what they were carrying, but knew nothing the interlopers could contrive would stand against the power of *Omah.*

In any contest between flesh and spirit, flesh must fail.

The shaman carried no weapon except his tomahawk and knife, used interchangeably for rituals and as his daily tools. They had been handed down from his grandfather to his father, then to him, the dagger's handle carved from bone, its blade honed to a razor's edge. It had claimed scalps before it passed down to Ohanzee, but no more. It was retired to that extent, its only bloodletting these days confined to ceremonies where his own was spilled.

More blood would soon be shed, the shaman knew, but not by him or his two warriors.

It was coming and he welcomed it.

A chance to purge the sacred land of maggots who defiled it and to see them on their way.

Migisi found the first purported signs of *Omah* three hundred yards due north of camp. He reined his tobiano pony in and waited for the other riders to collect around him, then directed their attention to his left, where two stout saplings had been bent and twisted so that one's branches were bound up with the other, almost like a braided rope, their bark split with the pale pulp showing through.

"What's this, Migisi?" Conklin asked.

"*Omah* does this to mark his territory," the Yurok replied. "It is a warning to intruders."

"Mythology," said Dr. Minninger, shifting atop his

palomino mare. "I can imagine half a dozen causes that might easily produce the same result."

Percy Manion chimed in to say, "Name one that makes good sense."

Flushing, the anthropologist replied, "I'd have to study all the evidence."

"Feel free," said Manion. "We've got time." When Minninger made no move to dismount, the hunter added, "What I see is no trace that the trees were clawed or otherwise disturbed by any animal that's native to these woods. Twisting means *hands,* Doctor, or something like them, and I wouldn't want to have these wrapped around my neck."

Minninger made a *humph*ing sound but offered no response. Jake Shandy, on his bay, was busy sketching in his notebook, trying for a simulation of the twisted trees. The others simply sat and stared, eyes shifting restlessly to scan the shadowed forest that surrounded them, as silent as a graveyard now, without a hint of birdsong in the air. Hands slid closer to the guns they carried, as if moving of their own accord.

"Well, it's a start," Conklin declared at last. "But not the creature we came looking for. Let's move along, shall we?"

Gideon Thorn thought that Migisi seemed reluctant to proceed, but the Yurok obeyed his paymaster and rode on, following a trail of sorts that animals had beaten over time, searching for food, water, or mating opportunities. The twisted trees aside, Thorn saw no evidence of any outsized creature passing on the track they followed, but he knew they must be drawing near the spot where Conklin's men had died so brutally.

Five minutes later, when Migisi stopped again, their animals were clustered on the fringe of what had been a sylvan forest glade. Today, by morning's light, Thorn saw the ferns and other bushes had been beaten down, some of them broken, and dark stains were evident on leaves, on grass, on mossy stones. Thorn didn't need a doctor to proclaim that they were copious bloodstains, the evidence of savage violence.

"It started here, apparently," Conklin informed the rest of them. "We don't know which of the three men was first attacked, but none escaped. One fired his shotgun, but you see there," Conklin told them, pointing to the scarred trunk of a great sequoia, "that both barrels missed their mark."

"The blood's all human, then?" asked Thorn, as half a dozen faces swiveled toward him.

Conklin cleared his through and answered, "We assume so. But without facilities for testing it..." He let the sentence die, then added, "Nothing...no one else...was found. I'm told that there were footprints, but it's rained since then."

Migisi scoured the clearing, finally surrendering and telling Conklin, "Nothing here."

"Then shall we go?" their leader urged.

Omah feels no need to impress its enemies, but it derives enjoyment from tormenting them and making them afraid. Fear is a feeling that it does not fully understand, being immune to it, but it observes the fright in smaller creatures as they die or flee from danger, and it understands that being frightened weakens those with which it must do battle soon. Fear clouds their minds and causes them to make clumsy mistakes that leave them open to attack.

And so, a little woodland music for the uninvited party stalking it.

In normal times, wood-knocking serves *Omah* as one

way of communicating with its own kind at a distance, less sophisticated than the grunting speech they sometimes share, but still effective for locating others, guiding them to prey, or warning them of danger on the wind. Against the small, pale ones, *Omah* has learned, the pounding causes tremors and disorients them—*mystifying* is another concept that eludes it, but it sees the physical effects and knows they can be turned to its advantage when the killing starts.

The branch it picks today is stout and strong, sprouting eight feet above the ground. Still, it is nothing once *Omah* has wrapped its hands around the rough wood near its base, tested its spring, and then applied its massive weight to dragging downward, barely noticing the strain before the limb snaps off and falls away. Another moment stripping it of twigs and needles, then it's ready to begin.

Omah selects a trunk, aged and partly hollowed out by time, insects, and woodpeckers that hunt them. Standing back, it hefts the freshly broken limb, then swings it sharply in an arc against the trunk, producing just the sound it hoped for, echoing through shady woods over a mile or more. A second swing, a third, and then it waits, head tilted, listening.

The first response comes from the west, two solid blows against another distant tree. *Omah*'s thin lips twist briefly in what might be called a smile. They have the hunters bracketed, not quite surrounded, but between two woodland drummers. That will frighten and confuse them, *Omah* thinks, which is a decent start.

It kills by daylight sometimes—deer and other, smaller animals for food when they are readily available—but when it stalks the pale two-legged things it much prefers darkness. Their eyes are weak compared to *Omah*'s, strained to capture images when there is no sun in the sky, and when they come carrying lights it rarely seems to help them.

Some night, *Omah* believes, it may be necessary to eradicate the trespassers entirely. It has seen the place where they take meals and go to sleep, with structures to protect them from the rain and snow in season. None of those will stand against the wrath of *Omah* when the time comes, when the first race to inhabit these vast forests rises up to cleanse its land of the infection carried by its enemies. Destruction of the trees, the land, its animals would stop, or *Omah* was prepared to spill the last drop of its own blood to achieve that goal.

And would it come to that?

Omah cannot imagine failure, much less the extermination of its tribe. The dark men who inhabit portions of its realm and leave it gifts of food outside their villages are allies of a sort, if not exactly friends. Both view the pale ones with suspicion and hostility borne out by time. Will the dark ones arise and help *Omah* eradicate their common enemy?

No answer comes to mind, so *Omah* swings the branch again and listens to its sharp report reverberate. Again, the distant answer comes back, swifter this time, ringing through the forest. *Omah*'s mind conjures an image of the hunters on their stick-legged animals, frozen in place and listening, trying to make out what the sounds mean, what their message may foretell.

A preview of destruction, rolling on the breeze.

"That's what the men tell me they hear, sometimes," Reginald Conklin said, head tilted as he listened to the distant rapping sounds. "Most say they heard it on the night their friends were killed."

"What could it be?" asked Abel Durst.

"*Omah,*" said Percy Manion in reply. "You hear it coming from two different sources, like the talking drums of Africa?"

"Oh, please!" said Dr. Minninger. "Are you imagining a tribe of monsters in the forest now?"

"Why not?" asked Manion. "It would go a long way toward explaining things."

"*Omah* is not alone," Migisi said, drawing the eyes of everyone about him. "Many stories from my people tell of two, three, even more of them walking together."

"Superstition," Dr. Minninger replied. "This seeing monsters in the forest—"

"And the pounding?" Manion challenged him. "What caused that, Doctor?"

"Well..."

"No, let me guess," the hunter cut him off. "Woodpeckers?"

"As a matter of fact—"

Manion's guffaw of laughter cut him off, bringing a flush or angry color to the anthropologist's jowls.

Conklin turned back to intercede. "Now, gentlemen—"

"I will not be made sport of by this...this..," sputtered Minninger.

"C'mon, Doc," Manion chided him, no longer laughing, but unable to suppress a somewhat mocking smile. "Woodpeckers? Why, they'd have to be the size of eagles to make that much noise."

"And your solution?" Minninger replied, his voice dripping with acid. "Must the sound be made by *monsters,* then? Some demon of the forest, never seen by man before?"

"My people see them many times," Migisi interjected.

"No, my friend." The doctor's tone had shifted from sarcasm to the edge of condescension. "What I meant by *man* was—"

"Careful, Doc," the circus hunter chided him. "Don't start a race war now by feeling all superior."

"I certainly do not," said Minninger. "It's simply that—"

"May we attempt to keep our purpose first and foremost in our minds?" Conklin cut through the argument. As if in answer to his words, another series of loud knocking sounds echoed from east to west and back again.

"If that isn't some kind of signal," Manion said, "I'll eat my hat."

"And what do you propose to do about it?" Conklin asked him.

"Wait until the sun goes down," Manion replied, "and have my traps in place. "Whatever this thing is—or what *they* are—it's still some kind of animal. Which means that we can trick it, one way or another."

"But if there is more than one?" their leader pressed. "What then?"

"Catch one and it can only go one of two ways," Manion replied. "The others run away, or they come in to help their pal."

"And if that were their choice?" Jake Shandy asked.

"Why, then, we drop the hammer on 'em and they're done. One's all that Mr. Barnum's paying for. It's all he needs."

EIGHT

They made the long ride back to camp in silence, for the most part, but for Percy Manion and Ham Stotler quietly discussing plans for *Omah's* capture as their horses traveled side by side. Thorn could have sidled close and tried to eavesdrop on them, but he thought he had already heard enough to understand what P. T. Barnum's hunters had in mind.

In short: one capture and a massacre.

It was a brutal plan, bagging one specimen for show and killing off however many others might come into rifle range. In fact, it was the first time Thorn had heard a concrete scheme for the annihilation of a species, or at least its representatives within a given area.

All that supposed that *Omah* was a living creature made of flesh and blood, of course, susceptible to traps and guns. So far, the evidence remained unclear. Three slaughtered men, some twisted trees, and rapping noises in the forest argued for an entity—no, make that *entities*—possessed of physical existence. And from Thorn's experience, if something lived and breathed, it could be caught or killed.

Against that evidence were legends spread by the Yuroks and other aborigines, describing *Omah* as a spirit or a demon capable of traveling great distances at will, appearing or evaporating as the need arose, and reeking havoc on the world of men while it was present in their sphere. Thorn's personal experience in Kansas, recently, would not permit him to rule out the spooky side of things, and if *Omah* should prove to be some otherworldly entity, it solved the problem posed by Percy Manion's plan.

Thorn could have told him that while ghosts could be destroyed, they couldn't be ensnared, confined, or shown off to the public for a dime per head.

Thorn had a problem now. He'd joined the Conklin expedition to assuage his curiosity about the murders and the legend of *Omah*, not to participate in the extermination of rare animals. He recognized a need to keep the loggers safe—and he had killed before, most recently in Texas, when a real-life monster threatened human life, including Thorn's—but that had been defensive action, not a calculated plan to wipe a species off the map.

So he opposed Manion's idea in principle, but how could he prevent it happening? And even if he blocked the circus hunter somehow, if *Omah* turned out to be a living, breathing creature, what prevented other showmen and their lackeys or a horde of trophy hunters from pursuing it?

Nothing.

If Thorn had not come looking for a chance to kill *Omah,* neither did he intend to make a lifetime's work of keeping it alive and well. That was ridiculous and totally beyond his capability. He could no more protect the animals of California from the human race than he could shift Earth from its orbit and attach it to some distant star.

Progress, as men defined it, would proceed no matter what he said or did.

He focused, then, on Percy Manion and the case at hand. If Thorn found *Omah* threatening a human, he would act accordingly. If not, there might be some means of frustrating Manion's scheme without provoking a blood feud between the two of them.

Something to think about, and maybe keep his fingers crossed, as long as it did not impede a trigger-pull.

Reginald Conklin heard the angry voices rising from his forest camp before the buildings were in sight. He spurred his leopard Appaloosa past Migisi's painted pony and could feel the others following, increasing speed as they drew closer to the woodland settlement. After his strange experiences on the trail, he dreaded what he might find waiting for him in the camp.

At first, only a mob of angry lumberjacks was visible, milling about, most of them armed with anything that came to hand. At sight of Conklin and the others riding in, the crowd surged toward them, jostling Ed Russell to one side before he had a chance to speak on their behalf. Still, Conklin kept his eye on protocol and called out to his foreman, voice raised to be heard above the babble of the rest.

"Ed, what's this all about?"

One of the others answered, bearded face upturned, contorted by his rage—or was it fear? "I'll tell ya what it is," he said, omitting "sir" or any other vestige of respect for his employer. "Injuns snuck in here while you was gone and left their marks all over ever'thing."

"He's right, sir," said Ed Russell, bulling through the

crowd until he stood in its front rank, to Conklin's left. "I can't say how it happened, but it's true enough."

Conklin frowned down at him. "Indians came into the camp unseen? In broad daylight, with guards posted? How is that even possible?"

A din of voices rose in answer, overriding one another, clamoring for his attention. Conklin sat astride his mount and raised his eyes, ignoring them until, at last, the babble died away. When they could hear him without Conklin shouting, he addressed them all at once.

"I'm speaking to your foreman now, the man in charge on my behalf. Until another of you is addressed directly, I expect a measure of decorum here, despite your agitation."

Some of them, Conklin supposed, were baffled by his words, but all would grasp his tone. Continued raving at the boss, after he'd called for quiet, would accomplish nothing but the shouters being handed severance pay.

"All right then, Ed," Conklin pressed on. "Explain."

"Well, sir, you all were gone an hour, maybe more, when Clem here"—nodding toward the red-faced, bearded man who'd shouted seconds earlier—"found markings painted on the north side of the mess hall. You can see 'em for yourself, sir. Not long after that, some others found more on the bunkhouses. I can't begin to guess how many redskins were involved, but they were deathly quiet. No one seen or heard 'em while they did their work."

"No one?" Conklin let just a touch of acid creep into his tone. "Who was on guard?"

"I've got the names, sir," Russell told him, gloomily.

"Then bring them forward." Conklin thought about dismounting, heard some other members of the expedition, dropping from their saddles, but he wanted to look down on the employees who had failed him.

Russell called out, "Decker. Johnson. Grantham. Howard. Front and center!"

Conklin eyed the four men who came forward, edging through the crowd of their coworkers, all four with the same hangdog expression on their faces, marking them as failures at a simple task.

"Well, men," he said. "Before I view the evidence, who wants to tell me what in hell prevented you from seeing vandals, red or white, creeping around the camp? Were you asleep? Drinking? If that's the case, I promise you have drawn your last red cent from Siskiyou."

The four were busy shaking unkempt heads now, each man mouthing variations of "No sir" and "Not a chance."

"All right. If you were all awake and sober," Conklin challenged them, "what happened?"

One of them—a burly logger in his twenties, sparse of whiskers on his long face—said, "It's like Ed told you, Mr. Conklin. We was on the watch, spread out just like Ed told us to, when Billy Green come runnin', yellin' about somethin' painted on the mess hall."

Green, the bearded man who'd spoken first, was nodding now, but kept his mouth shut.

From the other posted guards, it was the same: no one had glimpsed a prowler on the property, but after Green had spied the mess hall painting, others found similar markings on the bunkhouses. They'd armed themselves and fanned out through the woods, not daring to proceed beyond a hundred yards or so, and had found no one lurking in the area.

"I'll see this for myself," Conklin declared, and finally dismounted from his Appaloosa. "Mr. Russell, lead the way."

Gideon Thorn had never heard the Yurok language spoken, much less seen it written down, but as he stood behind the mess hall with the other expedition members, what he saw impressed him as the writing of an aboriginal, whatever tribe might be involved.

And make that *painting,* as the foreman had explained, since colors were employed, bright red and blue, the symbols interwoven in what could have been three words, each pictograph or letter twelve to fifteen inches high, irregular in size and spacing, daubed onto the log wall with decisive strokes.

Reginald Conklin called Migisi to his side and asked him, "Can you read this?"

After staring at the wall in silence for a full, long minute, their trail guide answered, "It is a warning, sir. To put it in your English tongue, it cautions, 'Leave or die'."

"Indeed!" Conklin had ruddy color rising in his face. "And is this your tribe's language, then?"

Migisi said, "Language is shared by other tribes: Chillula, Mita, Pekwan, Rikwa, Sugon, Weitspekan."

"And by Yuroks?" Conklin pressed him.

Followed, this time, by a silent nod.

"Show us the rest," Conklin commanded, and his foreman led the crowd to the first bunkhouse with its wall defaced, again in vibrant red and blue. The symbols differed, and Migisi translated the message on command.

"This one says 'Man cannot defeat *Omah*'."

"We'll see about that," Percy Manion told whoever might be listening, grinning with what struck Thorn as arrogance.

"The next one," Conklin ordered, and they moved on to

the second bunkhouse, where a shorter message had been painted. "Well, Migisi?"

"It says 'Death'," their guide replied, to angry murmuring from the assembled lumberjacks.

"And finally, the last," Conklin directed, trusting everyone to follow him around behind the final bunkhouse. There, they found three painted words, the first one in the seeming sentence matching what they'd seen at bunkhouse number two.

"Translate," Conklin directed, eyes shifting between Migisi and the wall.

"This one reads 'Death awaits you'," said their guide.

His words raised angry muttering among the loggers, some of whom appeared to blame Migisi for the vandalism, even though he'd been nowhere near camp when it occurred. The scourge of race again, rearing its ugly head.

Thorn turned away, returning Shadow to the stable, where he also spent some time with Bell. Their forest searching would resume tomorrow, but for now, he simply hoped Conklin could calm his crew and keep them out of trouble until night settled over the camp.

Ohanzee seldom complimented Coyote or Snake on anything they did. If they performed a task as ordered, it was simply what he'd planned and was expecting of them, nothing more or less. If they attempted some job he had set for them and failed, then it was grounds for scolding, at the very least. The shaman did not plead, cajole, or pamper his assistants, always feeling that the benefits of knowledge he bestowed on them should be reward enough.

On this occasion, though, Ohanzee *did* congratulate his

underlings upon a job well done. He'd seen the agitation spreading through the logging camp after they crept in, unobserved, and daubed their cryptic messages on walls of rough-hewn logs. It raised his spirits to observe the white men squabbling, clutching their pathetic weapons, while the forest at his back rang to the rapping sounds of *Omah* welcoming the hunters on their quest.

There would be no contact today, Ohanzee estimated. *Omah* needed time to plan its moves against the white men and had all the time required in which to plot its strategy. There was no rushing Nature or the spirits of the forest, anymore than he could hasten summer to arrive.

Tonight, perhaps, it would be different, but who could say?

"You both did well," the old man told his acolytes, watching them beam with satisfaction at his unexpected praise. Ohanzee instantly regretted it, suspecting that the compliment might lead to overconfidence next time he sent them to perform a piece of work—and in the present situation, that could get both of them killed.

Oh, well. As long as he survived to witness *Omah*'s vengeance on the white intruders, that was all that mattered. He could always find a new pair of disciples from the tribe, although its numbers were reduced and some of the young men remaining verged on the abandonment of their traditional beliefs.

Each time Ohanzee spun a prophecy, he found that fewer of his tribe believed or even paid attention to his words. Influenced by the white men and the changing world around them, some had fallen prey to bootleg alcohol, while others looked outside the tribe for wisdom and the fantasy of personal advancement in the cities where their kind were either shunned or given jobs so menial no white man would accept them.

It was shameful, but Ohanzee knew he had the antidote to dissolution of his tribe. With *Omah*'s help, he could reverse the deadly trend and make the Yurok strong again, lead them to purge invaders from their sacred lands, rescue their very homes from saws and axes in the hands of savages.

And then, perhaps, it would be time for him to rest.

Jake Shandy caught Thorn on his way back from the stable to his tent, one of his rifles in each hand. The heavyset reporter wore his normal smile, a questioning expression which, Thorn noticed, never seemed to reach his eyes.

"Some tricks today, would you agree?" he asked.

"Tricks?"

"Sure. The twisted trees, that knocking in the woods. Who do you figure set that up? So far, my bet's on Manion and that friend of his."

"How so?" Thorn asked, still on the move.

"Well, think about it," Shandy answered, keeping up with him. "Old Barnum needs a story for his new exhibit, whether Manion bags him something or they fake it with the carcass of an ape from Africa. Now they have witnesses to strange phenomena, and won't that get the rubes excited when they hear it from a sideshow barker?"

"So, you think...what? That the hunters went out early, or last night, to set this up?"

"Why not?"

"For one thing, they were with us when the knocking started."

Shandy shook his head and said, "I've got that covered. They could pay a couple loggers to sneak off and do their rapping trick, then scurry back to camp."

"And the graffiti?"

"Huh?"

"The painted messages in camp. Loggers again?"

"Could be. Or maybe redskins *did* creep in and leave the warnings. Works for me. They hate the logging company, as everybody knows."

"Sounds like you've covered all the angles," Thorn replied.

"I always do."

"Except for one."

"Which is?"

"The three murders that brought us here."

"Ah, well." Shandy had nearly lost his smile, but now it came back with a twist. "It's only murder if one person kills another, right?"

"Meaning?"

"I think some animal got hold of those three men. Not monsters from a heathen legend, something real. A grizzly, say. Maybe a mountain lion."

"You won't sell that to the other men in camp," Thorn said.

"*They* say. You've heard of Occam's razor?"

Thorn replied in Latin. "You mean '*Entia non sunt multiplicanda praeter neccssitatem*'?"

Shandy blinked at that. Said, "Maybe, if you're saying that among competing theories, the one with the simplest solution is probably true."

"That's the one."

"So we've got lumberjacks, okay? Uneducated men, at best, and half of them are foreigners. Some redskin fills their heads with fancy stories, then a bear or cougar comes along and mauls a couple of them—"

"Three," Thorn hastened to remind him.

"Two, three, what's the diff? Throw in the other tricks —knocking on trees, whatever—and the rest of them get heated up, jumping to the conclusion that some monster from the forest's coming to destroy them."

"Possibly," Thorn said. "Although you just told me that Manion and his friend were banging on the trees."

"*This* time," said Shandy. "When they heard the loggers talk about it, *click!* They get the bright idea to make it part of their performance."

"All for P. T. Barnum?"

"Who is paying them to find a monster for his show, or else."

They'd reached Thorn's one-man tent. He told the journalist, "Well, it's a theory, anyway."

"You think I'm wrong?"

"I think," Thorn said, "we'll have to wait and see."

NINE

The mess hall mood that evening, if not exactly solemn, was at least subdued. Most of the lumberjacks seemed tense, more so than on the day the hunting party had arrived, and as on that day, they showed up for supper bearing arms. The violation of their camp in broad daylight, with guards posted, had clearly worried some of them and angered others.

"I believe," said Percy Manion, sawing at a piece of meat that filled his dinner plate, "the tension in this room is thicker than my steak."

His sidekick, Stotler, laughed, a high-pitched sound that almost sounded like a horse's whinny to Thorn's ears.

Jake Shandy chimed in, singling out nobody in particular around the expedition's table. "Who thinks we'll have better luck tomorrow? Anyone?"

"I'm feeling confident," Manion replied, his mouth now full. "I'd say we're definitely close."

Shandy half-turned to wink at Thorn, then asked the circus hunter, "Based on what?"

"This thing we're tracking challenged us today. I've seen

it with big game before, in Africa and Asia. Tigers, for example, have an arrogance about them that demands a confrontation with a hunter. Even when they're caged, defiance lingers on."

"And you expect to cage this *Omah* creature?" Shandy prodded him.

"I have been hired to do so, and I've never failed at an assignment yet," Manion replied.

Shandy jotted a note, then turned back to his meal, still smiling.

That smile faded as a throaty, warbling howl echoed across the logging camp, cutting through conversations in the mess hall faster than the boss man could have called for silence. Almost instantly, another howl answered the first, its source uncertain beyond obviously coming from the camp's west side, while the first outcry issued from the east. Before the gathered loggers could react, a third inhuman voice rang out, this one apparently calling back to the others from the south side of the camp.

That did it for the lumberjacks, all springing to their feet, some overturning benches at their dining tables as they rose. Some of them faced the mess hall's entryway, a double door in the north wall, while others clustered at a smaller exit at the building's southeast corner. Most of those who had no guns were armed with axes, spades, or hammers. Those without a better weapon had drawn knives.

Before they had a chance to go investigate the sounds, or simply flee the hall, Reginald Conklin rose and shouted to be heard over their frightened grumbling. "Stand fast, men!" he commanded. "No one move! We face this threat together, if it is a threat, and get down to the bottom of it now!"

Gideon Thorn, now on his feet, hands resting on the curved grips of his matching Colts, wondered about the guards who had been posted in the camp outside while their companions gathered in the mess hall. He was turning back toward Conklin with the question on his lips, when one of those lookouts entered—bursting through a window near the mess hall's double doors and landing on the wooden floor.

Before the other loggers snapped and started screaming, Thorn had time to see the new arrival's head was twisted backward, wide eyes staring back over his own left shoulder where his neck had snapped.

Gaping aghast at the sprawled corpse of his employee, Conklin realized he didn't know the logger's name, nor those of any other lumberjack in camp except the foreman whom he'd trusted to control the operation from afar, while Conklin occupied his Sacramento office. Now, with any vestige of control about to vanish from the camp, Conklin suddenly felt himself a stranger in their midst, no reason any one of them should listen to him, when the threat of being killed was so much worse than simply being fired.

And he had come to supper in the dining hall unarmed.

Some distance down the table, to his right, he saw Gideon Thorn, at least, had come prepared. It was the first time Conklin had seen him with guns in hand, although he'd noted the twin pistols and the Bowie knife that Thorn wore on his belt. The weapons were not cocked or aimed as yet, but held against the young man's thighs, ready for use within an instant if a target should appear.

But none was visible as yet, only the dead man who'd

been hurled into the mess hall through the window, lying on his stomach, with his face turned toward the ceiling, mouth wide in a silent scream. Outside, the howling still continued, but it sounded closer now, more menacing, as if the former cries had shifted to a signal for all-out attack.

The stones came next. At first, when one thumped loudly on the mess hall's roof, Conklin imagined that some monster was atop the building, having leaped down from an overhanging tree. But when a second and a third fell rapidly out of the darkened sky, crunching against the rooftop shingles, he immediately understood the import of the sounds.

"Don't go outside!" he shouted to the frightened loggers. "Someone's lobbing—"

He was on the verge of saying "stones," when one of them—the size of an exaggerated pumpkin, or perhaps a watermelon—hurtled through the window shattered by his late employee, bouncing off the dead man's back and rolling on into the room. Absurdly, Conklin half expected to observe a note attached, but there was nothing, just a chunk of rock that would have killed the fallen logger if he wasn't dead already.

One of Conklin's men rushed toward the broken window with a new Winchester rifle, firing twice into the outer darkness without taking time to aim. As if on cue, the strange bombardment ceased, only to be replaced by further snarling, howling sounds that seemed to ring the mess hall.

"We're surrounded!" someone cried out from the ranks, lighting a fuse of panic in the rest.

"I've had enough of this," said Percy Manion. "Ham, come on." He spared a moment for the expedition's other members, rasping out, "Who else is coming with me?"

Conklin felt himself in motion, pushing through his nearly paralyzing fear to join the circus hunters. Thorn was circling the table, guns in hand, to intercept them, followed closely by Jake Shandy, but the rest seemed rooted where they stood, cringing as if they hoped to be ignored, become invisible to friends and foes alike.

Manion wasted no time reviling them as cowards, rushing toward the exit, shouldering his way through ranks of lumberjacks as if they weighed nothing at all. He reached the double doors in seconds flat and shoved them open, stepping out to meet the enemy. Behind him, heart wedged tightly in his throat, Reginald Conklin passed from lamp-light into night.

Thorn cocked his Peacemakers before he crossed the threshold from the mess hall into outer darkness. It was not completely black, of course: another bonfire had been lit beside the several empty tents, and lamps had been suspended from a scattering of upright posts, so loggers wandering about the camp by night wouldn't get lost or fall into the slit trench dug as a latrine. In fact, however, those lights only made the looming forest all around the camp seem darker and more menacing.

"Where are they?" Percy Manion asked the small cluster of men behind him.

"Better ask *what* are they," Reginald Conklin replied.

"Redskins," Ham Stotler offered, but he didn't sound convinced.

"It would've taken two, at least, to pitch that logger through the window," Manion said.

Thorn was already thinking *Omah,* but experience

prevented him from leaping to precipitate conclusions. He stayed quiet, checking out the shadows that surrounded them, guns ready for the first hint of a hostile move against them.

"Jesus, look at that!" Jake Shandy said.

They all followed his gaze toward where a stone had tumbled from the mess hall's roof and landed on the ground. Ham Stotler hastened to it, bent to pick it up, and grunted, "Damn thing must weigh close to eighty pounds."

"I don't see two men pitching that onto the roof," Manion replied. "Too awkward."

"So, a monster?" Shandy asked him, faithful notebook open in his hand.

"Nobody's saying that," Conklin cut in. "Don't put words in our mouths."

"I wouldn't, sir. But—"

"If we're going after them," said Manion, "there's no time to waste."

"Go after *who?*" asked the reporter. "Go which way?"

A gunshot from the north side of the camp appeared to solve the latter problem. As a single man, they rushed in that direction, found another of the posted lookouts crouching, rifle pointed toward the forest straight ahead of him.

"What is it, man?" Conklin demanded.

"Something ... I don't know ... running that way." He jabbed the rifle forward in a pointing gesture. "More than one, but ... I don't know ... so *big*."

"We need torches," said Manion. "Ham, snap to it! Every second wasted now give them a greater edge."

Stotler croaked "Yessir" and ran off somewhere in search of torches, leaving Thorn to wonder if such things were even ready made and waiting in the camp. Apparently they were, or Manion had himself prepared them, for the hunter's sidekick soon returned with four in hand, already lighting one and using it to set the others blazing as he came.

"That's better," Manion said. "Now, as we start, is everybody armed?"

"I'm not," Conklin replied.

Thorn half-considered handing Conklin one of his twin Colts, then quickly changed his mind. Instead, he told Conklin, "I've got you covered. Stick with me."

And even as he spoke, Thorn hoped that offer wouldn't prove to be the kiss of death.

Abel Durst remained inside the mess hall when the lumberjacks poured out into the night, standing beside his cold, unfinished supper with the anthropologist from Washington and Caleb Heaton, their physician for the quest that had become a waking nightmare.

"Should we go and join the others?" Heaton asked.

"Not me," said Dr. Minninger. "I came to supervise a so-called scientific expedition, not to chase madmen around a forest in the dark."

"Madmen?" Durst challenged him.

"Who else do you suppose attacked the camp? Whether it's loggers gone berserk or Yuroks drunken and delirious on firewater, this clearly has a human explanation."

"You seem mighty sure of that, for someone who won't step outside," Heaton replied.

"It's simple logic, *Doctor*," Minninger half-snarled at using Heaton's title. "Surely you, a man of medicine, do not believe in forest demons?"

"Right this moment," Heaton said, "I couldn't swear to what I think."

"Preposterous! If such things did exist—"

Durst never heard the rest of Minninger's pronouncement, as an ululating cry from somewhere in the outer dark drowned out his stiff, pedantic voice. The anthropologist swallowed whatever he had planned to say and sat down on the bench beside their table, reaching for the knife beside his plate as if it offered safety from attack.

"Does that sound like a man to you?" Durst asked him.

"Lunatics are unpredictable," said Minninger. "They howl like animals and sometimes eat their own—"

Another shriek, this one more like a woman's scream of mortal pain, prevented Minninger from saying any more about the strange proclivities of lunatics. Instead, he huddled down into himself and held the knife in front of him as if it were a talisman. Durst snatched his own up from the table, but it felt inadequate.

Whatever wailed and waited for them in the night would not be thwarted by a simple blade.

"We can't just stay here," Durst announced. "At least, *I* can't. I'm going out to see what's happening."

"Don't be a fool!" Minninger chastised him. "The only thing you'll find out there is injury or death."

Durst rounded on him, pointing toward the dead man who had crashed in through the mess hall window with his head twisted around backwards. "And do you feel safe sitting here? Are you secure against whatever's raising hell outside?"

"I. Won't. Go. Out," Minninger bit off each word in turn, spitting them off toward Durst.

"Then stay," the bureaucrat replied, surprised at his

own anger and the impulse that propelled him toward the open double doors, accelerating as he covered ground.

"Wait up!" called Dr. Heaton after him. "I'm coming with you."

Neither of them waited to see Minninger, still planted on the bench, glaring in fury at them, finally deserted in the dining hall, rising to follow with reluctant steps, as if en route to an appointment with the gallows.

And they weren't alone, Durst saw, as he emerged. Most of the lumberjacks were milling in the open space between the mess hall and their bunkhouses, a dozen anxious conversations overlapping, here and there a braver man trying to rally others for an organized defense and getting nowhere with it. They were on the verge of snapping, chaos waiting in the wings to sweep them every which way if they started running for their lives.

And then the roaring started, like a pride of lions from his left, the west side of the camp. A second later, someone opened fire, a rifle cracking in the night, its muzzle flash marking the battle line.

Behind Durst, Dr. Minninger muttered, "I *said* we should have stayed inside."

Howling in the deep, dark woods continued as the torchlight searchers slogged their way from camp, northward, but what had changed? To Thorn, it seemed the cries became more distant as they traveled, weapons at the ready, and diverged from due north to the east and west. He understood the laws of physics from his Harvard studies and was not convinced the creatures they were hunting could have moved so far, so quickly.

"Anybody else hear that?" he asked his three companions.

"What?" Manion demanded, in a surly tone. He didn't bear frustration well and clearly thought they should have sighted *Omah* by that time.

"The calls," Thorn answered. "When we started from the camp they were in front of us, maybe two hundred yards away. The cries we're hearing now are farther off, coming from east and west at once."

The others paused to listen, torches raised to drive some of the shadows back. After a moment's silence, more howls echoed through the night and Manion muttered something underneath his breath.

"What's that you say?" asked Conklin.

"It's a trick," the hunter said again, but this time loud enough for all of them to hear.

"Explain," Conklin replied.

"You heard me!" Manion fairly spat. "A trick—or a diversion, if you like. We see it often in the field, from roosting birds on up to big game animals. Most of them don't just stand there waiting for a bullet. Once, in India—"

"Stick to the present, if you don't mind," Conklin said.

"All right. We know there's more than one of these damned things, whatever they turn out to be. That's obvious from how they hit the mess hall, right? Nothing on Earth can lob stones from two directions at once, and it explains the murdered lookouts, too. How three armed men got taken down without putting a scratch on even one of their attackers. They were ambushed!"

All of them were on alert now, Thorn with a Peacemaker cocked in his right hand, a bright torch in his left. Ham Stotler dropped to one knee, while his sawed-off shotgun's double barrels swept the night. Manion was carrying a double-barreled rifle, larger than the Sharps carbine that Thorn had left behind.

And at the moment, none of it felt adequate.

"So, what are you suggesting?" Conklin prodded Manion.

"They've been drawing us away from camp," the hunter said. "I can't say whether they intend to pick us off or simply lead us on a merry chase, but either way, smart money says some of them stayed behind."

"Behind?" Conklin repeated it, as if his mind was missing the connection.

"At the camp," Thorn said.

And at that moment, gunshots echoed from behind them, to the south, from the direction of the logging camp or very close to it.

"You see?" Manion seemed almost thrilled that he'd been proven right. "A trick!"

"What are we waiting for?" Thorn asked the others, and without pausing to see if any of them followed him, began to run, his senses on alert for any traps as he retraced his footsteps toward the battlefront.

TEN

"White men are fools," Ohanzee said. "They do exactly what we wish them to."

"Not many left the camp, Old Father," Apisi pointed out.

"Because they are cowards, as well as fools," the shaman answered. "Never mind. The brave ones take our bait. The rest are easy game."

"Will *Omah* kill them all tonight?" Askook inquired, a bit too eagerly.

"*Omah* will do what it must do," Ohanzee said. "I summon it but am not privy to its thoughts."

That silenced his companions for a short while as they stood in darkness, watching five men armed with guns and torches hiking northward from the logging camp. Behind them, all around the damaged dining hall, more stood and jabbered in their uncouth tongue, most of them armed in one way or another, staring at the night beyond the reach of their bonfire and hanging lamps. The woodland night was vast, and they were trapped within it, cut off from the nearest white man's city by a full day's travel and surrounded by an enemy they could not see, much less begin to understand.

"We could slip in and strike them now," Coyote said. "Set fires and watch them run. Pick off a few while they're distracted."

"Do not be foolish like the whites," Ohanzee cautioned him. "This fight is *Omah*'s. It is not for us to interfere."

"But—"

"Disobey me at your peril, child! Respect *Omah*'s ability and do not make yourself a target when it is inflamed by combat with the enemy."

"No, Old Father."

Though Apisi feigned contrition, Ohanzee could see his true heart, and he knew the young man was frustrated, anxious to become a full-fledged warrior, often heedless of the risks involved. If not restrained, he might be dead by now, and that would be an inconvenience for the shaman as he sought another youth to do his bidding.

"It is almost time," Ohanzee told his two companions.

He could not read *Omah*'s mind, but simple logic told him that the searchers who'd left camp had traveled far enough by now, trailing the decoy sounds that *Omah* used to lure them away. Meanwhile, tall, silent shadows darker than the forest night had moved in closer to the logging settlement, preparing for a push that might convince the interlopers—or, at least, the number that survived—to quit this land and seek their fortunes elsewhere.

Did Ohanzee hope in vain? Perhaps. But what was life worth if a man forsook his dreams?

Nothing at all.

"What is it waiting for?" Apisi asked through gritted teeth.

"Patience!" Ohanzee hissed at him. "Without it, you will never make a hunter, much less any kind of warrior."

"I am sorry, Old Fa—"

Ohanzee raised a hand for silence, cutting off the strained apology. In front of them, perhaps two hundred yards away by white men's reckoning, *Omah* had once again begun to snarl and howl. The crowd of frightened loggers visibly compressed under that sound bombardment, still blind to the looming shadows that drew closer by the moment. When the moment came, none were prepared to save themselves, and yet they fought, the roar and muzzle flashes of their scattered firearms scarred the night.

"May we not join in now?" Apisi whined.

Ohanzee fought an urge to slap him. Told the disappointing youngster, "Watch and learn. For now, that is your task."

Dr. Theo Minninger was terrified. The roaring sounds and gunfire made him tremble to the point he feared that he might soil himself, the ultimate humiliation in the presence of so many country bumpkins who would doubtless laugh at him. He felt like bolting back inside the mess hall and barring its door behind him, to hell with all the others left outside.

In fact, he had begun to turn and slink away when Abel Durst reached out and caught his arm. In startled reflex, Minninger almost retaliated with the steak knife he was carrying, but stopped himself a heartbeat short of lashing out.

"We're safer here," Durst cautioned him.

"That proves you've lost your mind," Minninger answered through clenched teeth.

The forest night was perilous. One man had died already, screaming in the dark before his mutilated body hurtled through a window, cast aside like garbage. Minninger pictured himself as the next victim, ripped asunder by whatever was surrounding them, howling and shrieking in the darkness just beyond their fires.

Monsters? Impossible. His pricey education told him so.

A sudden urge to laugh came over Minninger, no doubt a symptom of hysteria. It sprang from him, remembering his declarations from the moment he had learned about their expedition, speaking with such great authority on subjects he could not begin to understand. His doctorates in anthropology and archaeology were worthless here and now, for all their stylish script and scrollwork, certifying the exalted knowledge demonstrated by Theophilus Xavier Minninger. Even the pompous name, used only on the title page of books and scientific papers he had written, mocked him now.

Useless, he thought, and cursed himself. *I should have stayed in Washington.*

Now he might die, ripped from his comfortable life by something unimaginable, a demented creature that belonged in children's storybooks, not raging in the night around a rustic logging camp. And when it came for him at last, would he possess even the basic minimum of courage needed to defend himself in vain?

He tugged against Durst's grip and felt it slacken, as the bureaucrat whispered, "All right. Go back inside. If you want to sit in the mess hall like an invalid, so be it."

Stung at some level where pride survived, not yet gone numb, Minninger cursed and held his ground, clutching the puny knife he'd brought along, leaving his partly-finished meal behind, the food now cold and never to be eaten. The short knife was better than a bare fist, Minninger supposed, but not by much.

A few more shots were fired into the darkness, aimlessly, achieving nothing, while the roaring sounds persisted and redoubled. Finally, the foreman—whatever his name was—seemed to change his mind about the wisdom of confronting unknown enemies outside, without the benefit of solid walls surrounding them.

"Head back!" he told the loggers. "Get inside right now!"

Minninger did not wait around to be told twice. He bolted for the open doors and ran back to the table he had occupied before Durst nagged him into venturing outside, sat down where he had been short moments earlier, and wrapped both hands around his knife as if it were some kind of a protective talisman.

Durst and the loggers followed in a rush, crowding into the dining hall with guns and other makeshift weapons at the ready, nearly every man among them babbling like an auctioneer, with no one listening.

Durst tugged one logger's sleeve and nearly got a back-hand for his trouble, recognized at the last moment by the bearded man who growled, "The hell you want?"

"What's do you think that is, out there?" the bureaucrat inquired.

"Got no idea," the lumberjack replied, eyes wild beneath a set of bristling brows. "They's comin' back!"

Oh Christ, Minninger thought, *don't let me die here, not like this.* He was not praying—had, indeed, swapped science for religion decades earlier, without regret—but still the old words came to mind in his extremity.

Wasted.

No one could save him now, as vicious howling rent the night outside and something heavy, something *hungry,* threw its weight against the mess hall's double doors.

Gideon Thorn had always been athletic, from his grade school days through Harvard, and he proved it now, outrunning Conklin, Percy Manion, and Ham Stotler—whom, he noticed, only now, limped slightly when he ran, though not at normal walking pace. Thorn kept a pistol in his right hand, torch gripped in his left, and counted off the loping strides that would return him to the camp.

Hoping he wouldn't be too late.

Gunfire from that direction was a ragged, uncoordinated sound. The lumberjacks weren't soldiers, trained to fire by ranks and stand their ground against an enemy attack. Thorn pictured them in flight, looking for any cover they could find, wasting their ammunition on wild shots at shadows, barely aimed. How many of them would survive until he reached the site, and how could he assist them?

Thorn still had no idea what they were up against, whether his guns would serve or not to ward off an attack, but they were all he had, beyond his skills at hand-to-hand defense. And from what he had seen so far, a husky man flung through a window with his neck twisted, Thorn didn't fancy squaring off against *Omah,* much less an angry group of them.

Now he glimpsed the first lights from the camp and slowed his pace, in case the raiders—whoever or *what*ever they were—had posted lookouts of their own. He would not put it past a group of creatures capable of laying siege to Conklin's camp and taking down its guards. The only questions now involved *Omah*'s strategic cunning and the number of opponents they must face.

Thorn cleared the camp's outskirts without encountering a trap and fired his Colt Peacemaker once into the air immediately, as a signal to the loggers and a warning to their foes. The central bonfire was already dying, and the lamps hanging from poles cast long shadows around the tents erected for members of Conklin's hunting party. Twenty yards in front of Thorn, two bulky shadows rose among the tents and fled, lumbering toward the treeline at a pace surprising for their size.

Thorn fired again, this time in earnest, as his running targets reached the trees. A throaty yelp from one of them suggested he had scored a hit, but neither of them slowed, both vanishing into the night as Percy Manion's rifle boomed and sent a useless bullet flying in pursuit.

"Two of them!" Manion blurted out. "And did you see the size of them? They're huge!"

"Not only two," Thorn contradicted him, moving with slower, cautious strides as he approached the mess hall. As he neared the structure, muzzle flashes blinked from two of its windows, bullets fired high and wild into the night. More hulking shadows circled there, one with its arms upraised and something in its hands, prepared to hurl it as a missile.

Thorn squeezed off another shot and saw the creature drop whatever it was carrying. It ran, trailed by at least two more, although there could be others on the far side of the mess hall that he couldn't see. Manion squeezed off another hasty shot and evidently missed again, from the profanity that followed his attempt.

"Inside the mess hall!" Thorn called out now. "Hold your fire!"

After a heartbeat's hesitation, someone on the inside said, "They're back! Come on!" A moment later, shaken-looking lumberjacks began emerging from the dining hall, scanning the camp with haunted eyes.

"You sure they're gone?" one of them asked. Thorn recognized him as the foreman, Russell, carrying a Winchester.

"For now," Thorn said. "But I don't know how long."

For safety's sake, they crowded back inside the mess hall, feeling better with the walls and lamps around them, plus a stout roof overhead. Thorn didn't try to count the loggers present, since he'd never heard a final tally of how many occupied the camp, and any total he came up with would be meaningless. While Thorn replaced his three spent cartridges with live rounds from his belt, most of those present started talking—make that *yelling*—all at once, demanding answers from their boss. Off to one side, Thorn spotted Dr. Heaton tending to a pair of lumberjacks whose shirts were torn, revealing bloody wounds.

Ed Russell turned on the excited loggers, raising his voice over theirs, demanding order from the frightened mob. "Shut up, goddamn it! Nobody can understand you if you're all talking at once!"

It took another minute, give or take, but the excited, shouted babble died away to *sotto voce* grumbling from the ranks. At that point, Conklin climbed atop one of the long and sturdy dining tables, looking out across the upturned faces, and addressed his men.

"I won't pretend to know what's going on out there," he told them, one arm pointing toward the nearest shattered window. "Coming back, the four of us saw *something,* but I couldn't put a name to it."

"*Omah,* one of the loggers answered back.

"Monsters," another said. "Don't matter what you call 'em."

"Fair enough," Conklin replied. "The good news is, we've run them off, at least for now. One of them, I believe, is wounded, thanks to Mr. Thorn."

Eyes shifted toward him, the expressions ranging from anxiety to grim suspicion. None looked grateful for whatever Thorn had managed to accomplish, if indeed he had done anything at all.

"All right," Conklin pressed on. "It's obvious we can't get any work done under these conditions, but I promise you, you'll all be paid for any time lost at the normal rate, until this problem is resolved."

"Problem?" somebody echoed. "Hell, we's gettin' killed!"

"I understand that," Conklin granted. "And the families of those who've fallen shall be compensated, I assure you. In the meantime, we must band together and eliminate this menace with dispatch. Agreed?"

If Conklin was expecting cheers at that, the silence of his captive audience must have been disappointing. Somewhere near the back, a voice called out, "Or we could just high-tail it outa here!"

"You can," their boss replied. "And God speed to you, wherever you're headed. It's a day's hike southward through the forest, to Yreka, and I can't begin to guess where you might find another town. Of course, you'll be out on your own. Rifles and tools belonging to the company stay here, defending life and property."

"I say we try it anyhow," the same voice said. "Who's with me." No one spoke or raised a hand, until the one who'd planned on fleeing growled, "Well, shit! I guess I'll stick."

"All right, then," Conklin said. "We stay, and first thing in the morning, take this battle to our enemies. We track them down and—"

"What about the missing men?" another voice called out to interrupt him.

"Missing men? Who are they?"

"Elmo Hutchins," someone said.

Another shouted, "Billy Dane."

"Two of the guards," Ed Russell told his paymaster. "We didn't pass 'em, coming in."

Conklin nodded and told the crowd, "Our first order of business, then, at first light in the morning. We locate the men and render any aid we can."

First light, Thorn thought, and figured they were already too late.

Sleep was in short supply for the remainder of that night. No one assigned to tents trusted the flimsy canvas shelters to withstand attack, preferring safety in the mess hall over lying virtually in the open air. Before he settled down, or tried to, Thorn took his Winchester and made the short walk to the stable, checking in on Shadow, Bell, and other animals collected there. He soothed them all the best he could, with gentle words and thoughts, pleased and a bit surprised to find them suffering less agitation than the humans who believed themselves superior to all "dumb animals."

When he returned, loggers had fortified the dining hall as best they could, nailing plywood over the broken windows, bringing in a heavy, rough-hewn beam to bar the double doors from the inside. Thorn looked around the place and knew he would feel more secure inside it than reclining on the hard ground in his pup tent, but some others didn't seem to feel the same.

Worst off, from what he saw, was Dr. Minninger, sitting alone with hands clasped in his lap and rocking slightly on the bench he occupied, lips moving as he muttered something to himself that Thorn couldn't make out. Minninger waved off Dr. Heaton, but let Abel Durst remain beside him, not quite close enough to touch, whispering something to the anthropologist in an apparent bid to calm his nerves. It was bizarre, watching the man from the Smithsonian break down that way, and Thorn could only wonder if his usefulness to Conklin's hunt was at an end.

Was that how someone looked when their most strongly-held beliefs were proven wrong, and everything they claimed to know with blind, unswerving certainty was snatched away from them?

How would *he* act and feel if *Omah* held the secret to his family's annihilation, twenty-four years earlier? It seemed unlikely, even now, but Thorn had long since learned not to predict the outcome of a quest before he reached its final end.

Without that mystery to spur him on, what would he be? What would he do to fill the days remaining in his life, young as he was? Instead of answers, all Thorn saw before him was a yawning void.

He shook it off and settled into checking out his

weapons before lying down to sleep. Danger and its attendant mysteries did not affect him as they did the expedition's other members—certainly not as destructively as they had shaken Dr. Minninger. Thorn was accustomed to the risks posed by his search for answers in the darkest corners of the West, and would not be the one who bolted when the stakes were raised.

This time—not for the first time—he was playing in a game where they were life and death.

ELEVEN

APRIL 22, 1876

Thorn managed several hours' sleep and woke to Saturday's first light, intruding on the darkened mess hall from around its doors. Some other members of the expedition were already up and moving, Reno Lofton getting busy with his pots and pans, stoking the stove. The only one who seemed reluctant to get up was Dr. Minninger, lying beneath one of the trestle tables, knees against his chest in a fetal position, the fingers of one pale hand clutching a knife.

Already gone, Thorn thought, wondering how Reginald Conklin planned to deal with one of his authorities, now visibly disabled. He supposed that Minninger might wake, fully recovered, ready for the hunt, but at the moment it appeared unlikely.

Either way, Thorn knew, the problem wasn't his.

He had his own agenda for the hunt, which could be satisfied without bagging a trophy specimen of *Omah,* but some contact with the creature—whatever it was—might be required. And if the answer he procured was not the one he'd hoped for, Thorn would simply have to live with it.

Breakfast was rushed but good enough. Ed Russell went to hail the loggers who had spent the night in barricaded bunkhouses, while Lofton whipped up scrambled eggs aplenty, griddle cakes, and ham for anyone who had an appetite after the night they had survived. When Russell came back with the lumberjacks who felt like eating, Thorn heard him tell Conklin that they'd lost some men during the night.

"Lost?" Conklin challenged.

"Runaways. There was no sign of anything snatching 'em up."

"Cowards." The boss man shook his head. "I wonder if they're still alive by now?"

"Don't matter," Russell said. "I wouldn't waste time looking for a runner, anyhow."

"Nor me," said Conklin. "When we're finished here, we need a burial detail for those we lost last night."

"Just one, so far," Russell replied. "As for the missing men, I just don't know."

"We'll find out soon enough." Conklin observed Thorn listening, Jake Shandy coming up beside him with his notebook poised, and asked them both, "Will you be coming with us when we take the trail this morning?"

Thorn answered with a silent nod, while Shandy said, "I wouldn't miss it for the world!" Too much enthusiasm masking fear, perhaps, or was he simply dedicated to the quest for a sensational headline?

"What will you write about us?" Conklin asked the newsman.

"Can't say I've decided yet," Shandy replied. "There's so much to take in, and who'll believe it, anyway?"

"The whole world," Percy Manion offered, joining them. "At least, after they've seen an *Omah* in the flesh."

"You still sound confident," Shandy replied, "despite last night."

"They caught us unaware," Manion answered, frowning. "It won't happen again."

"So, you intend to stay awake and watch around the clock?"

"I'll do whatever must be done. And at the moment, that means eating."

Thorn and Shandy passed along the serving line together, took their heaping plates back to a table in the dining hall's far corner, and began to wolf their food without time spent appreciating it. It tasted fair enough and went down easily, the only things Thorn cared about right now.

What really mattered to him was what happened next: the hunt resumed and one more chance to solve a mystery the ancient forest hid from prying eyes.

"Three more dead," Ohanzee told his men, and almost smiled. The half-grimace was so unusual that Askook found it almost ghastly.

"There would be more if we had joined the fight, Old Father," said Apisi, sounding glum.

That almost made the shaman snort. "Oh, yes. And you might be among them. Then would you be pleased?"

Coyote blinked at that, as if he had been slapped. "I only meant—"

"I know exactly what you meant," the old man interrupted him. "When I was your age, I, too, dreamed of battle as the ultimate fulfillment of my life. Today I'm old and have learned better. You should ask the Great Spirit for wisdom now, before it is too late."

"They only know about one logger dead, so far," Snake said.

"The other two will be *Omah*'s surprise for them," Ohanzee answered, "though the dullest white man must already sense that they are gone."

Through trees and from a distance, barely visible, Ohanzee saw the hunters getting ready for another trip into the forest. They were armed, mounting their horses, one man leading two mules laden down with gear concealed by canvas wrapping. At a distance from the mess hall, others were engaged with shovels, digging graves.

Soon, they would need more holes than there were living men to excavate them.

And that prospect made Ohanzee smile again, with all of his remaining teeth.

"What shall we do when they set out?" Coyote asked him cautiously. "More painting on the walls?"

"No," said the shaman. "They are on alert now and would surely see you. We shall follow them into the forest and observe what *Omah* has in store for them."

That made the younger would-be warriors smile, as well.

"I hope the spirits feast on them," Snake said.

"It's possible," Ohanzee mused, although he wondered if the forest demons might be sated from their meal last night. Were beings of the spirit realm subject to all the laws of nature that encumbered common men?

"I'd like to taste them, too," Coyote said, surprising both of his companions.

"Careful," warned Ohanzee. "If you stray too far along

that path, you may become *wendigo* and your soul is lost forever."

Hearing that, Apisi lost his vulpine smile and ducked his head in recognition of his error. "Thank you, Old Father. I have heard the tales, but doubted whether such a thing is truly possible."

"My people dealt with a *wendigo* once, many summers before your birth," Ohanzee said. "His given name was Keme—'Thunder' in our language—and he was impetuous. One winter, on a hunting trip, he and a friend were trapped by snow. Before the thaw, Keme was all alone, but he returned to plague the village as a monster, physically insatiable. He slaughtered several kinsmen before young braves of the tribe managed to capture him and purge the curse with fire."

Snake and Coyote pictured that, the screams and leaping flames, until Ohanzee's voice returned them both to present-day reality.

"The hunters leave," he said.

Seven whites on horseback this time, with their Yurok guide, trailing two mules behind them. They were headed north once more, as on their previous excursion from the logging camp. This time, five of them carried long guns, plainly visible, ready for action at a moment's warning.

Would the weapons help them?

Ohanzee had never heard of any man defeating *Omah,* much less killing it. He could not say with any certainty if that were even possible, but *if* it happened, he would be on hand with his companions. They would join the battle then, without a second thought, and give their lives if need be for their people, for the sacred land that they revered.

"Come," he instructed, and began the long walk that would probably consume most of his day.

The better part of two hours elapsed before they found the missing loggers—or, in this case, what was left of them. Thorn couldn't have identified them, since he'd never met them personally, but Ed Russell knew them by their garb, and by a tattoo on one corpse's severed arm.

"That's Billy Dane," he said, a slight catch in his throat, examining the first man's mutilated body from his seat atop a silver dapple mare. "I know that hand-tooled belt, together with the knife he carried."

"Never had a chance to use it," Percy Manion noted.

Thorn couldn't decide which wound had finished Dane. His skull was split and emptied out, as if someone had scooped his brains out of the cranium, but both arms had been torn out of their sockets, making him resemble something from a giant's tug-of-war. His legs were still attached, but with the trousers mostly ripped away, large bite marks on his thighs and calves.

"Hell of a way to go," Jake Shandy offered.

"Christ, I hope he didn't feel all that," Ed Russell said.

Conklin distracted them, asking, "So this is Hutchins, over here?"

"Elmo," the foreman said. "Yes, sir. You see the arm tossed off beside him, there? I'd know that tattoo of the island girlie anywhere."

"Was he a sailor at one time?" Shandy inquired.

"Nope," Russell answered. "But he always talked about it, shipping out to some faraway land where it was always warm and sunny, sand and palm trees, willing women who would give you anything without a second thought."

"Mutiny aboard the H.M.S. *Bounty,*" Shandy said, and then seemed startled when the others stared at him, uncomprehending. "What? The ship! Some of you must have read the story. Sir John Barrow published it in 1831, about the mutineers that seized a vessel on its way home from Tahiti back to England, in the 1780s. None of you?"

Thorn had read it for a class at Harvard, but he didn't say so now. Reginald Conklin cleared his throat and said, "If we may focus on the present for a moment..."

"Sorry," Shandy said. "I only thought...Tahiti...and you said...forget it."

"We should search the area for evidence of what did this," Conklin continued. "Any sign at all may well prove useful."

"I'd say there are too damn many signs," Manion remarked. "Something's trampled the whole clearing to hell and back, the footprints overlapping one another till they're useless."

Thorn dropped from his saddle and began to scrutinize the ground more closely. Manion was correct, in part: the footprints overlapped, distorting one another for the most part, as if savage celebrants had danced around the two dismembered men in some demonic ritual, but there were places where enough remained of one print or another to suggest their size and form. The tracks that Thorn picked out were large—none less than fifteen inches long, by his rough calculation—and were more or less in human form, complete with five toes, arch, and heel. At one point, near the corpse of Billy Dane, he also found a massive handprint in the forest loam, nearly identical to any normal man's except in size.

Manion was looking upward, toward the trees, and frowning as he said, "I can't see putting up our nets around this clearing. They're not big enough, for one thing, and we'd have to climb too high."

"Perhaps it's just as well," Conklin replied. "I feel our first duty is to return these poor unfortunates to camp, and bury them together with their murdered friends."

"We've still got lots of daylight left," Manion replied. "Most of the day, in fact."

"Ride on, then, if you choose. But I insist on rescuing what still remains of these fine men."

"Your call," the hunter said, not bothering to mask his sigh. "Ham, fetch the canvas from the mules so we can wrap 'em up."

The ride back to the logging camp was solemn, nearly silent, each man in the single-file procession watching out for movement in the trees that might suggest a trap. They made it safely, after all, and found a grim crowd waiting for them, most eyes on the gory bundles bound atop the pack mules, leaking through their canvas shrouds and staining Percy Manion's nets.

"Can't hurt," the hunter told his aide at one point. "Smell of human blood might draw them in quicker than any bait."

Two open graves were waiting for the butchered guards, but no one had the stomach for arranging their remains in anything resembling normal order after all they'd suffered. Thorn detached himself from those who stayed to watch the holes filled in, prayers mumbled over mounds of earth, and two more wooden crosses mounted with a shovel serving as the hammer that would drive them home.

No one felt much like lunch when they were done, though it was getting on toward noon and Reno Lofton had been busy cooking in the mess hall. Thorn managed a small steak with potatoes on the side and washed it down with mediocre coffee, listening while Conklin and the circus hunter argued over whether they should press the hunt that afternoon or leave it for tomorrow. Conklin favored the delay, while Manion made the point that fresh game trails demanded speedy action.

"If we set the traps today," he told Conklin, "we have a decent chance of snaring one when they come back to camp tonight."

"You say 'when'," Conklin challenged him. "Should there not be some question of their imminent return?"

"You think so?" Manion countered. "After what they did last night?"

That silenced Conklin for a moment, while Manion pressed on. "As far as they're concerned, this camp is nothing but a happy hunting ground. They've killed *six* of your people now, and gotten off without a scratch as far as we know. Maybe Thorn, here, winged one of them last night, maybe not."

Thorn didn't hear a question in there, so he concentrated on his meal. Conklin, he saw, was weakening. Having committed to the rescue of his logging camp, he clearly couldn't think of any reason to postpone the hunt.

"All right," he said at last. "As soon as everybody's finished here, we'll go back out again. But I expect results, Mr. Manion."

"And so does Mr. Barnum," said the hunter. "I intend to satisfy you both."

With lunch out of the way, the hunting party hastened to get ready for its second outing of the day. Migisi was already waiting with his pony, while the others saddled up and fetched their guns. Shadow seemed ill at ease, but Thorn managed to calm the stallion with a gentle word and soothing thoughts, although it still seemed apprehensive as it eyed the woods around the logging camp.

Jake Shandy was the only member of the party who appeared to be unarmed, but Thorn recalled the sawed-off pistol hidden in his coat pocket. Manion, having missed that conversation earlier, asked whether Shandy felt entirely safe. The newsman answered back, grinning, "I have a pen, though and that's supposed to beat a sword."

"Tell that to *Omah*," Manion groused.

"Be glad to, if I see him." Turning to face Thorn, he added, Or should I say 'it'?"

"I'm still not clear on that, myself," Thorn said.

"Well, if you don't mind, I'll stick close to you. I've noticed that you're handy with those shooting irons of yours."

"I manage," Thorn admitted. "Just don't stand in front of me or get too cozy, if there's gun work to be done."

They set off as they'd traveled previously, single-file and saying little while the forest giants closed about them, cutting off most of the sunlight that had played across the camp. Dead leaves and needles underfoot muffled the passage of their horses and the mules behind them, while the riders felt constrained to limit conversation to the minimum. Birdsong greeted them as they began their journey, but it faded as the bloody clearing came in sight once more, as if the very creatures of the forest held their breath.

"See what I mean about the clearing?" Percy Manion asked them all together. "Just not suitable for putting up our nets over the killing ground. I see a couple game trails, though, that might serve better, if the things we're tracking travel over them."

"It shouldn't be that difficult to tell," Thorn said.

"You're right. Let's have a closer look and see if we can work with what's available."

"These nets of yours," said Conklin. "Are they stout enough for what you have in mind?"

"I've captured lions, tigers, and a polar bear with nets just like them," Manion answered. "If we get a good drop on the target, it'll be wrapped up just like a Christmas package, good and proper."

"Hmm. I wish I shared your confidence," the logger said.

"Oh, ye of little faith," Manion replied, laughing. "Just leave the capture to the experts. When we've bagged one for the show, I reckon that the others will come sniffing after it, to see what's going on. When that happens, my friends, it's each man for himself."

TWELVE

Omah smells men and instantly experiences several sensations, coming almost simultaneously. First, its hair bristles from head to hips, a primal warning of potential danger, even through the puny creatures that occasionally cross its path have never harmed one of its species yet, and may in fact be physically incapable.

Next, as its nostrils twitch, seeking the pungent, frequently offensive odor of mankind, the creature trembles slightly—not from fear, oh no, but from anticipation of the contact still to come. It can track men by their scent alone, although its eyes are sharp, and its intended targets are so clumsy in the woodlands that they leave innumerable signs for searching eyes.

By nature, *Omah* is an omnivore. It eats whatever comes its way, from nuts and berries up to fish and rodents, deer that it can capture or finds dying in the forest, even bear if one surprises it from time to time and combat is inevitable. It prefers a peaceful life, and being left alone, but lately that has not been possible, with noisy humans bent on ravaging its ancient home.

Omah has not been summoned by the darker men, as they seem to believe. It is impervious to chants and prayers, except to watch them from the forest shadows while contorted figures leap and dance around a blazing fire. They are amusing in their way, and they have never interfered with *Omah*, fleeing from its presence when their paths cross, sometimes carving effigies of hairy forest-dwellers on their totem poles or leaving food out for the giants who, though rarely, creep into their villages by night.

It is the pale men who have roused *Omah* to anger and provoked a gathering to drive them out by any means required. Their hacking, sawing sounds and cries of "Timber!" herald brute destruction of *Omah*'s homeland, its hunting ground, the place where future generations have been spawned since ancient ancestors first stepped onto the continent and started moving southward, fanning out. All that around the same time dark men came by the same path, and long before the first pale faces gazed upon the western ocean, claiming everything they saw for nations that *Omah* would never visit, never dream or understand.

They are enemies, and that is why their scent, their sounds, inevitably make *Omah*'s mouth water. If it has to kill the interlopers, why not make a meal of them, as well?

Nature provides.

Now, after being taught a lesson just last night, the parasites are back, no doubt with some new plan to make *Omah*'s former pastoral life a misery. That calls for a response, in force.

It finds a sturdy fallen limb and hefts it, tests its weight, then picots toward the nearest looming tree and swings.

Setting the traps was more complex than Thorn had first imagined: climbing trees adjacent to the game trails, then hauling the nets aloft, securing them ten feet or so above the ground, then rigging lines that would release them when a man or other creature of substantial size passed underneath. Ham Stotler did most of the work, while Percy Manion urged him on with various directions from below and saw the traps arranged precisely to his liking, first on one game trail, and then the other. When the work was finished and the hunter satisfied, each net was posed above its own selected pathway like a giant spider's web.

The wood knocking began almost as soon as they were done. The first blow startled Thorn and set him reaching for his Winchester, soothing Shadow with gentle thoughts and words. The stallion wasn't troubled yet, but he could not predict how it would act if roaring creatures suddenly began attacking through the woods. His best bet: be on board by them, ready to flee.

Which posed a problem, since he couldn't simply leave the others to their fate. Migisi would escape, Thorn reckoned, and he had few qualms about the circus hunters who had come to make a profit on a species they had never seen. Reginald Conklin and Jake Shandy, on the other hand, were relative babes in the woods, unaccustomed to fighting for their lives against uncertain odds. Ed Russell was more rugged, and had clearly been around and seen his share of action. He might slip away or go down fighting to defend his boss, whichever struck him as the thing to do.

As for the others, though, a knack for boardroom savvy or a clever turn of phrase would not protect them from determined predators. And while Thorn had no personal responsibility for either man in that event, he had attached himself to their endeavor and now felt a need to help them if he could.

The first knock, although sounding distant, froze the other expedition members in their tracks. All conversation ceased immediately, as they cocked their ears and waited for whatever might come next.

Another knock, farther away, but definitely answering the first. Thorn knew, after last night, that it was no coincidence. More followed, spread throughout the forest to their north and west, advancing slowly by the sound of them, as unseen drummers homed in on the clearing where two men had died so horribly last night.

"They know we're here," said Manion, almost whispering.

"How could they?" Conklin asked him.

"Smell, sight, hearing, take your pick. They're animals, remember, with a range of senses far beyond our own."

"We should retreat then," Conklin answered back. "Clear out and give your nets a try." A tremor in his voice revealed the boss man's fear.

"If we have time," Manion advised, clutching his double-barreled rifle. It resembled one that Thorn had seen before, in Boston, behind glass in a gentleman's club where the walls were adorned with the heads of exotic species. Large enough to bring down anything, he thought, unless it broke the shooter's shoulder first.

More hammering, and it was definitely growing closer now. Thorn mounted Shadow, steadying him, with the stallion's reins in his left hand, Winchester in his right. He didn't think the wood-knockers were close enough to strike their party yet, but still Thorn had to wonder: what if there were others creeping through the forest silently, while Conklin's team focused upon the noise?

"I want to *see* them," Manion muttered, slowly edging closer to his brindle gelding with reluctant steps, eyes on the forest all the while.

"Catch one," Ham Stotler answered, sounding nervous now, "and you can watch it all day long. Right now, I'm thinking we be in the trap."

"Don't be a coward!" Manion snapped at his companion. "We've faced worse than this."

"I don't recall it," Stotler muttered.

"The Watusi, when their blood was up. Remember that?" Manion urged him.

"But they was *men*," Stotler replied, "not *monsters*."

"Ham, there's no such thing as monsters," Manion told him. "Only animals that we don't understand yet."

"Well, *these* animals will rip us limb from limb," the sidekick said. "I'm gettin' outa here!"

Before he had the chance though, a stone lofted from the shadows, barely visible before it fell, and struck him squarely on the head.

"The fighting has begun again," Ohanzee told his two young warriors. "Shall we try to watch?"

Apisi took the leap. "And possibly join in, Old Father?"

"Your time is coming," said the shaman. "I shall tell you when and where."

Apisi masked his disappointment, barely, and fell into step behind Ohanzee, Askook bringing up the rear, as they moved closer to the white men whom, they all hoped, would be slaughtered soon. Wood-rapping echoed through the forest all around them, but it held no terror for the

Yuroks, long accustomed to placating *Omah* with their rituals.

Ohanzee was prepared. He wore a knife and ornate tomahawk, used more for ceremony than for battle, and it had been years since he last took the warpath against other men—in fact, before the whites arrived. His adversaries had been Maidu then, and Konkow, with occasional raiding by Wiyots until they were taught respect. All were his brothers now, as Ohanzee considered them, allied in spirit against the encroaching white men who would rob them all of everything and leave them homeless, starving, if their progress was not curbed.

And to prevent them taking over, Ohanzee had placed his trust in *Omah*'s hands. Whether the forest giants would reward him for his prayers, or if they only fought for selfish reasons of their own, he was not sure and did not care. As long as they observed a common purpose, and the Yurok did not act in such a way as to bring retribution down upon themselves, Ohanzee would be satisfied.

But he could not deny his tomahawk craved action. After all those years of inactivity, its blade was thirsty for the taste of blood again. Men's blood, that was, and who better to sate it than the whites who had invaded and despoiled his people's land? If he should die in battle at his age, what higher honor could Ohanzee wish upon himself?

Yes, it was tempting, but a shaman's sacred duty said that he should set a positive example for the young men of his tribe: no drinking firewater to rot his brain, no rank dishonesty or immorality, and no encouragement of futile actions that would bring dishonor or destruction down upon the tribe he served.

Before Ohanzee went to war again, one last time, he must know within his heart that he could win, or that there was no other choice. And that, he knew, depended in large part upon *Omah.*

Stotler's slouch hat and bushy hair beneath it cushioned him somewhat against the falling stone, but it was large enough to stun him even so, and start a crimson trickle worming out from underneath his hatband, down across his crooked nose. He took one backward stagger-step, then sat down hard, blinking, red-faced, trying to figure out why he had lost his balance.

"Wha...what?" he demanded of the others, as if one of them had struck him.

Percy Manion shouted, "Watch yourselves" and raised one arm above his head, presumably to shield his skull. Instead, the fist-sized stone that struck him found his chest, rebounding with a solid *thunk* of impact while the hunter managed to remain upright, though clearly shaken by the blow.

"God*damn* it!" Manion raged. "You want a fight, then show yourselves!"

The expedition's other members were less anxious for a confrontation, focusing on self-defense. Thorn's first thoughts were for Shadow, swinging up into the stallion's saddle where, he thought, a rock aimed at the horse stood roughly equal odds of striking him instead. He drew his right-hand Colt at the same time, scanning the forest shadows for a hostile target worthy of a shot, but finding none.

Whoever or whatever the stone-throwers were, Thorn gave them top marks for their use of camouflage. He only saw the rock they aimed at him when Shadow's startled thought alerted him, in time for Thorn to lean back in his saddle while the stout projectile whispered past his face.

"Thanks, boy," he said aloud, and didn't care who heard it as the rain of stones continued. One struck Conklin in the hip; another sent Migisi ducking low; a third hammered Ed Russell's shoulder as he climbed aboard his silver dapple mare, but he still managed it and swung the horse's nose toward camp, cursing a blue streak at the sudden pain.

"Clear out!" The order came from Percy Manion, urging them to do what all were trying now, Manion himself still clambering to mount his brindle gelding.

Conklin, hampered by the sharp blow to his hip, managed to climb aboard his leopard Appaloosa, shouting, "Hiya!" as he rode past Thorn and Shadow, back the way they'd come into the forest, man and horse alike wild-eyed.

Thorn played follow the leader, urging Shadow to a gallop behind Conklin's stallion, Migisi falling into line behind them on his tobiano pony. Russell wasted two shots on the silent woods, no longer ringing with the wood-knock echoes, then high-tailed it in Migisi's wake back toward the logging camp. Manion succeeded in his scramble for the saddle, then unsheathed his Winchester and covered Stotler as his sidekick struggled upright, moving fumble-footed toward his rubicano mare, and hauled himself aboard with straining effort. As they fled the glade together, leaving Seamus O'Leary to his frightened mules, the hostler cursed them raggedly, but quickly got his animals in hand and led them braying from the danger zone, chasing the other riders back toward camp.

But would they make it?

Thorn had picked up hostile emanations from the forest, sentient minds embroiled with savage thoughts that still possessed a fair degree of clarity. The thinkers—more than one, although he couldn't positively pin a number down—were bent on punishing the hunters, either driving them away or killing them, whichever proved to be the easiest and most effective tactic.

Thorn discerned a plan. He could not feel specifics of it, but he knew a trap when he saw it and shouted up the narrow forest trail to Conklin. "Wait! Slow down!"

And in another heartbeat, knew the warning came too late.

A branch, drawn back and held by unseen hands, suddenly whipped back into place, struck Conklin in the chest, and swept him back over the Appaloosa's rump, tumbling into the middle of the narrow trail. He landed heavily, ass over teakettle, and lay where he had fallen, an obstruction in Thorn's path.

Gideon reined in Shadow, only yards from trampling Conklin in the dust. He clutched the reins in his left hand, Peacemaker in his right, and waited for the next attack while other riders, coming up behind him, fought to slow their animals in time.

"They tricked us!" he called back along the trail. "Be careful now, and don't shoot one another by mistake."

In front of Thorn, Reginald Conklin stirred, showing erratic signs of life, and slowly struggled to all fours, gaping around him, stunned by double impact from the branch and falling from his horse. Trying to speak, he said, "I don't...I didn't..." then got lost in whatever he'd planned to say and gave it up, scrambling across the game trail like a wounded spider as he tried to stand erect.

"Watch out," Thorn cautioned him. "They're all around us."

As if verifying that announcement, rapid wood-knocks started up again, much closer now and sounding furious, their speed and urgency heightened. At the same time, another stone flew out of nowhere, striking Conklin on the head. It sent his rolled-brim Stetson sailing, with a plume of blood from Conklin's open scalp, before Conklin collapsed again, sprawling across the trail. His horse ran on toward camp, heedless of having lost its rider.

Thorn immediately holstered his Peacemaker, whipped his lever-action rifle from its saddle boot, and jumped down from his mount, aiming a slap at Shadow's rump and willing it to leave him where he stood. The stallion spared a look at Thorn, then bobbed its head and ran on, after Conklin's leopard Appaloosa, hammering along the trial back toward the logging camp. Thorn trusted it to get there safe and sound, convinced the enemies who had surrounded them were after men, not animals.

Cocking the Winchester, he moved to Conklin's side and helped the logging magnate to his feet. Behind them, spry Migisi had released his pony, crouching with his own rifle and eyeing forest shadows as he looked for living targets. So far, none of the attackers had revealed itself, but from the furious vibrations Thorn experienced, he guessed that it would not be long in coming.

And when that began, what chance did any of them have?

Thorn wondered now if he'd been foolish, letting Shadow flee without him, but he stood by his decision. As he steadied Conklin, rifle buttstock braced against his hip, Thorn sent his own thoughts out into the forest, trying to be accurate and not to let his fear control him. He had been in tight places before, and either talked or fought his way out to the other side, but this was different.

This time, his enemies remained invisible, and he could barely touch them with his mind: enough to know that they were present, and intently focused on their human prey, but not enough to change their course of action.

"Stand and fight!" he warned the others. "It's your only chance!"

And then, another rain of stones began.

THIRTEEN

Ohanzee's heart was pounding. At the first sharp cracks of gunfire, coupled with unearthly screams, he started running with a vigor that surprised himself and his younger companions, racing past Snake and Coyote, both of them laboring to keep up with him. The shaman had no memory of reaching for his tomahawk, but it was in his right hand now, his hunting knife clutched in the left.

He had surrendered logic in the frenzy of the moment, hearing white men shout and cry aloud for help, their forest adversaries bellowing in anger as they closed in on their prey. Ohanzee knew that it was foolish, that it might be his last act on Earth, but he wanted to be with them at the kill.

Apisi and Askook were grinning as they ran a step or two behind him, breathing heavily, bemused to see the old man pulling out in front of them, weapons in hand. For all his warnings to abstain from contact with the whites, he'd found the fighting spirit one last time and it had taken over, giving him the speed and courage of a warrior in his prime. Neither considered challenging the change of heart, as anxious as they were to join the fight.

Ohanzee heard the tone of howling from the forest change as he drew nearer to the ambush site. Instead of simply roaring out defiance now, the *Omah* were communicating, closing in around the hunters who were arrogant enough to challenge them on their home ground. He wondered, fleetingly, what would become of all the white men back at camp when these were dead, but then decided that it hardly mattered. Whether they all fled or stayed to die among their cabins like trapped animals, the word would ultimately spread. More whites would come—it was their nature to advance, consume—but they would know that something terrible awaited them.

And they would walk in fear.

Nearing his goal, Ohanzee knew that victory might be impossible for Yurok tribesmen, even with the mighty *Omah* fighting on their side. Unlike his tribe, there was no end of white men waiting to invade new territory, thousands of them pressing toward the western sea, crushing all obstacles of Nature underneath the sheer weight of their greed. If thousands died, then tens of thousands would replace them, swarming like insects, infesting everyplace they found.

Ohanzee's people would be overrun in time, inevitably, but at least they had a chance to leave their mark behind and earn a place in history, perhaps even in legend. And although he recognized the foolishness of his attempt, the old man would be first to strike a blow against the surging enemy.

Ohanzee felt that he had earned that right, simply by living to his present age and witnessing the slow decline of all that he held dear.

More gunshots now, and they were close enough to stab Ohanzee's ears like heated needles. He ignored Snake and

Coyote, did not care if they gave up and ran away or followed him to momentary glory. They were nothing to him now, no longer acolytes or students to be tutored, simply an encumbrance if they slowed him down.

How sweet it was to feel that fire again, and know that even Death would have no sting.

Gideon Thorn was fighting shadows, getting nowhere fast. He had already fired his Winchester four times, at shifting targets in the forest gloom, only to see them duck aside each time, apparently unscathed. He held his fire now, ducking stones that hurtled past him from the shadows, hearing grunts of pain from his companions as a rock struck home.

All seven members of the hunting party were still on their feet and fit for action, more or less, but several had suffered injuries as they retreated from the slaughter clearing in the forest, toward their camp. Reginald Conklin limped, from where a flying stone had struck his hip. Ham Stotler, still bleeding from underneath his crumpled hat, was less than steady on his feet. O'Leary had a nasty gash across one cheek, the eye above it swelling shut, but he had managed to propel his mules toward camp and held an old six-shooter ready, just in case one of their enemies revealed itself.

Thorn had abandoned any thought that they were human, even though the glimpses he had caught in passing showed him creatures walking upright, with the basic form of men: two arms, two legs, heads mounted on broad shoulders without any necks to speak of, barrel chests and squared-off torsos, all covered with hair or fur. He had not seen their faces yet, but guessed from sounds they uttered that they would be apelike, similar to pictures he had seen of African gorillas and chimpanzees.

But it was their *size* that troubled Thorn the most. He understood that shadows warped perception, but he would have bet his life that none of the attackers measured less than seven feet in height, with some closer to eight, or even nine. Weight was a guess, under the circumstances, but he pegged the smallest of them he had seen in passing at four hundred pounds or better, little of it being fat to slow the creatures down.

And they *were* creatures, Thorn was satisfied, not Yurok warriors on the warpath. Size alone proved that, together with their dearth of weapons and the sounds they made, nothing Thorn could discern as spoken language. Still, it was the *feelings* he received from them that finally made up his mind—the waves of rage, determination, even sparks of fear—that he would not receive from any human being, only animals.

And what did that make *Omah,* finally?

Thorn honestly had no idea.

There were no apes in North America, according to the science books he'd pored over in school, unless you saw one in captivity, shipped overseas or up from somewhere in the steaming Amazon Basin. Their appearance in the wilds of California, if confirmed by capture of a specimen, would call for a revision of those texts and all of scientific theory that preceded them. As for creation fables, well...

A stone that must have weighed five pounds flew past his face, and Thorn responded with a rifle shot in the direction it had come from. Still no solid target, but if they could hold the enemy at bay while they retreated slowly toward the logging camp, they just might have a chance.

And after that?

Again, no ideas came to mind.

Thorn crouched to make himself a smaller target, wondering how far he had to travel yet, before he and the others reached their goal—and which of them would make it to thc camp alive.

"Come on, you bastards!" Percy Manion bellowed. "Show yourselves!"

He knew it was a waste of time and breath, talking to animals, but rage and fear had driven him to what some fancy doctors called a breaking point, where it was difficult to grasp the difference between reality and fantasy. He knew the rifle in his hands was real, likewise the roaring forest shadows that bombarded him and his companions with a rain of stones, although he still had no idea of what they were, in fact, or how to classify them on a scientific scale. He knew they had the best part of an hour's hike to reach the logging camp, and that his traps, so carefully prepared, were likely useless now, with their intended prey pursuing Manion and the other members of his party as if they were prey, not hunters with superior intelligence.

Infuriated by the stark reversal of his normal role in hunting wild things for the Barnum circus, Manion almost felt it when his mind snapped and the forest colors changed before his eyes. He really *did* see red, a new experience for him, though he had heard the old expression for a fit of anger countless times before. This was a real sensation, as if all the trees around him had begun to bleed, tingeing the undergrowth and shifting shadows they concealed with deep crimson. It seemed to Manion that he saw his brutish enemies more clearly now, that he could separate them from the other forest shades and finally accomplish what he'd come to do.

His first attempt, a hasty shot at one of the attackers, proved to be a wasted effort. Cursing, Manion blamed himself for firing while the target moved and he had no clear shot from where he stood. The answer to that problem, he divined, was crystal-clear.

He must get closer to the beasts and try again. Once he had dropped one of them, Manion told himself, the rest would flee to save themselves.

Reloading his double-barreled rifle swiftly, Manion marched directly toward the treeline where his adversaries hunched and moved, it seemed, with virtual impunity. His brisk advance would startle them and, hopefully, provoke one into meeting him, accepting Manion's challenge. Just to help his odds, he shouted at the creatures, heaped invective on them that would sound like gibberish to wild ears, hoping that his tone itself would signal willingness to fight.

When he had covered half the distance, someone grabbed his arm. Manion spun on his heels to find Ham Stotler gaping at him, mouthing words that took a heartbeat to interpret.

"Boss, come back!" his sidekick said. "You can't go runnin' off like this."

Snarling, Manion responded with a butt stroke from his weapon, dropping Stotler to the ground with blood smeared on his startled face, as red as their surroundings seemed to Manion's eyes. Before the fallen man could protest, Manion turned away from him and rushed the trees, excited when he saw one of the looming shadow-shapes detach itself and stride to meet him.

"There you are!" he crowed, and raised his rifle for the

kill shot, but a long arm swept it from his grasp and swung the firearm as a club, crushing the hunter's skull and turning all his claret visions into deep, impenetrable black.

Migisi thought his time had come. It was not everyday that spirits from the old tales came alive and put on flesh, attacking men for violating Nature's laws. He knew the story of *Omah* and its importance to the Yurok people, but to see the thing itself take living form—not one, but many of them, all hostile—was almost more than he could comprehend.

And now, Migisi feared that revelation meant the last day of his life had come.

Like any other Yurok, he was more or less prepared to die—not looking forward to it, certainly, but having made his normal daily peace with spirits of the land, water, and forest. There was nothing more for him to do, but face Death bravely and display no fear to shame himself before his ancestors.

Migisi saw one of the white men die—the hunter, Manion—and it seemed to him a simple, almost painless end. Whatever happened to the lifeless body later, whether *Omah* left it otherwise untouched or gnawed it to the bone, the dead man's spirit had already flown to its reward or punishment beyond the earthly realm. Migisi didn't know or truly care what happened to a white man's spirit when he died; their strange and contradictory religious told so many different stories, he had long since given up on trying to untangle them. Right now, he only knew that Percy Manion was no more, and he might be the next to fall.

But he would go down fighting. There was no alternative for any Yurok warrior.

So Migisi knelt and pumped the lever-action handle on his Winchester. It might be futile to resist *Omah* with force, but what choice did he have? At least this way, his ancestors would know he died a man, and not some mewling, fearful child.

The creature that had brained Manion still held the hunter's rifle by its barrel, fresh blood dripping from its wooden stock. It raised its eyes from Manion's corpse and found Migisi sighting down the barrel of his Winchester from twenty feet, an easy shot despite dusk's advent, on a target so tall and wide. Its lips peeled back, and from its throat emerged a roar that terrified Migisi, though he dared not let it show.

Omah was charging at him now, still roaring as it cleared the ground between them with its swift, long strides. Migisi fired a shot and saw it strike below one of the creature's rough, dark nipples, then he tried to fire again, forgot to work the lever-action in his fear, and cursed himself for his foolish mistake.

All the more startling then, when two more bullets struck *Omah,* one in the throat, the second punching through an eye socket, the monster tumbling forward, sprawling prone with outstretched hands less than a yard from where Migisi knelt.

Behind him, one of the white men—Gideon Thorn—levered another round into his rifle's chamber as he said, "I think it's time we started making tracks."

All right, then, so the creatures *could* be killed. Thorn felt no satisfaction from it, as he watched Migisi spring erect and hurry past him with a muttered word of thanks, but it was better than continuing to fight against opponents that might be invincible.

He followed in Migisi's wake, first jogging backwards, watching as the other creatures hesitated, eyeballing their fallen comrade, then he turned and ran, seeing Jake Shandy up ahead of him, and Russell helping Conklin keep a decent pace despite his injured hip. Stotler had lagged behind, crouching beside his boss's corpse. Seamus O'Leary, having freed his mules and fled, was nowhere to be seen.

"Come on, Stotler!" Thorn cried, and hesitated, hoping Manion's aide would snap out of his trance and make an effort to escape.

Stotler half-turned to stare at him, blinking, then called, "I can't just leave him here."

"We've got no choice," Thorn said. "The two of us can't—"

He was interrupted by a blur of motion from the tree-line, something flying through the air, and Stotler took his second head wound from a heavy stone. This one, Thorn saw, caved in the left-rear quadrant of his skull and doused the light of life behind Ham Stotler's eyes, like blowing out a lamp. The small man toppled over, limp, his body masking Manion's mutilated skull and face.

Thorn ran, no one alive behind him now to call for help. The *Omah*s were advancing cautiously, all on alert and conscious that they'd lost a member of their raiding party, deep-browed eyes on Thorn as he retreated from them, casting frequent glances back across his shoulder. They were focused on him now, the man who'd killed one of their own, and what would that mean if he fell into their hands?

Revenge immediately came to mind, and risky as it was, he paused for just a second, opening his mind to any signals that the creatures might be sending out, even unconsciously. The only thing he found was pure, blind rage.

And it was time to run as if his life depended on it—which, in fact, was now the case.

Thorn gave it everything he had, knowing his stride and speed could not match that of his pursuers. They were gaining on him, steadily, inevitably, till be swung around and triggered two quick rifle shots to give them pause. No hits, but looming shadow figures ducked away from Thorn's .44-40 slugs to save themselves, mindful of what the rounds had done to their companion moments earlier.

Thorn saw his chance and took it, pouring on more speed while his pursuers were diverted by the gunfire. How much farther to the logging camp? He smelled wood smoke, or was it his imagination giving him false hope? Another hundred yards he hoped, or two at the outside, and he would see—

A heavy stone struck Thorn between the shoulders and he fell facedown into a bed of rotting pine needles and leaves.

FOURTEEN

Ohanzee reached the battle site and found two white men dead, their skulls crushed, bodies trampled by the *Omah*s after death. One had a ragged bite, the size of two hands, ripped out of his neck and shoulder, but the corpses had escape the mutilation that Ohanzee normally expected from an *Omah* kill. The creatures had not stopped to feed, and now his ears were telling him the battle had moved on, the other white men fleeing while the *Omah*s doggedly pursued.

Snake and Coyote overtook him in the clearing, winded as Ohanzee was, despite their younger age. The shaman took a moment to collect himself, then nodded toward the sounds of gunfire south of where they stood, in the direction of the logging camp.

"They run but cannot get away," he said, surprised to hear the breath wheeze in his throat. His mad dash through the forest had exhausted him, and while Ohanzee tried to catch his second wind, the two young braves were clearly growing restless, anxious to be off and running with the hunt.

Did he have strength to join them? It might kill him, burst his aged heart, but now Ohanzee felt a grim determination to proceed at any cost. He'd come this far, rallied the demons against white intruders. It would shame his ancestors if he dropped out now, near the finish, just because his body had begun to fail him.

"May we follow, Old Father?" Apisi asked, trembling from pent-up energy and anger.

"May we?" echoed Askook, through clenched teeth.

Ohanzee bobbed his head and took off in a shambling run. The two braves could have passed him easily, but matched his pace out of respect, no matter how it frustrated the pair of them.

A few more yards, and then the shaman stopped again. This time, it was not age or weariness that halted him, but rather what he saw lying across their path: the long corpse of an *Omah*, clearly brought down by a gunshot to the head.

His two companions gasped as one, surprised. "How can this happen, Old Father?" Snake asked.

Ohanzee pondered that, shaking his head, before he answered, "Possibly, the old magic has failed. White medicine may be the death of us. *Omah* may not have strength enough to drive our enemies away."

The younger braves looked stricken, almost on the verge of angry tears. Apisi answered, "No! I don't believe it. We must help them, Old Father!"

"Help them!" Askook echoed.

Ohanzee saw his own death then, without specifics, but clearly enough for him to know the time was drawing near. It was not frightening at his age, rather something of a personal relief.

"Help them," he said, as if the notion had begun with him. "Yes, we must try."

Or die with them, he thought, *here at the ending of an age.*

"This way," Ohanzee said, and he began to run once more, beyond all feeling now, focused upon the moment when he found the whites again and faced them as he would have in his youth, trading in life and death.

Gideon Thorn struggled to rise on hands and knees, his spine aching, ears buzzing from the blow that knocked him down, and waited for the end. While groping for his Winchester, convinced there'd be no time for him to use it, he could only hope that ending would be swift and relatively painless. Let the monster known as *Omah* crush his skull, or snap his neck at least, so that he wouldn't feel whatever happened next.

Instead, a rifle show rang out above his head, sounding as loud as thunder, and a strong hand hauled him upright as if he weighed nothing. Seconds later, he stood eye-to-eye with grim Migisi, long and tangled hair framing his face.

"Life for a life," the Yurok said. "Now we must go."

And saying that, their guide squeezed off another rifle shot, aiming along the way they'd come after the forest ambush. Thorn turned with his own weapon in hand, to see an *Omah* stop and shake itself, blood splashed across one of its massive shoulders. Not a fatal wound, by any means, but still enough to slow it down and force some hesitation on the hunter's part.

Thorn raised his Winchester, prepared to take the one shot that he knew might kill the beast, then hesitated, peering over rifle sights into the *Omah*'s eyes. Despite its simian aspect, those eyes were nearly human, bright with understanding and intelligence behind the anger that controlled it for the moment.

Once again, Thorn sent his thoughts instead of lead, trying to pierce the creature's shield of perfect rage. Devoid of words he guessed the thing would never understand, he tried to frame a peaceful image: man and *Omah* standing side by side, if not the best of friends, at least not brawling enemies. The image in his mind held on for six or seven seconds, then the creature snarled and lurched toward Thorn, along the narrow trail.

Thorn fired, but not to kill, dropping his sights and aiming for one of the *Omah*'s thighs, nearly as big around from Thorn's perspective as Migisi's waist. The bullet found its mark, more blood erupted from the wound, and the *Omah* dropped to all fours, howling in pain.

Sorry, he thought, as if conversing with the beast, *but it can heal.*

Condolence wasted, Thorn followed Migisi as the Yurok fled back toward the logging camp. Deserted by his normal sense of passing time, Thorn hardly knew if they'd been running for ten minutes or an hour. He knew dusk was coming, closing in, with full night close behind it, always faster to arrive deep in the forest, where huge trees screened out much of the sunlight every day.

If they had still not reached the camp by dark...

A night alone with *Omah* in the forest would mean death.

Knowing the creatures had a weakness—that they could be wounded, even killed—did not relieve Thorn's mind. He had the strength of will to slay *Omah* in self-defense, but it felt *wrong* to him, regardless, as it might to shoot a stranger who was simply trying to defend his land. Men had been slaughtered, yes, and brutally, but Thorn could not help thinking that it was the humans' fault somehow. The arrogance that made Conklin and others claim the right to clear-cut virgin forest without even taking time to find out who or what inhabited the land repulsed Thorn. If their circumstances were reversed and Thorn felt threatened by invaders in his home, how else would he respond?

Instead of waiting, looking for another target on the trail, he ran.

"No one's ever going to believe this," said Jake Shandy, panting. "If my editor will even run it, anyone who reads it will be calling me a drunk or worse."

Reginald Conklin drew a ragged breath and said, "Not if we show them one of these damned things, alive or dead. They won't be laughing then."

"And how are we supposed to do that?" asked the foreman, Russell. "Case you missed it, boss, those circus fellas Barnum sent you are as dead as dirt, the two of' 'em."

"I didn't mean to put the creatures on display," Conklin replied. "But if we kill one, or it's knocked unconscious somehow and we tie it up..."

He'd seen Manion and Stotler died, horrific, but his mind had quickly shifted, even while Conklin was running for his life, expecting to be killed at any moment. *What about the circus money?* he was thinking. Tens of thousands, from the stories he had heard, which would go far toward putting Siskiyou Logging back in the black, despite its losses to a tribe of monsters. And beyond the money, he'd be *famous,* written up in books, journals, and newspapers around the world.

Conklin would be the man who'd found the Missing

Link, by God. Who else on Earth could make that claim? He could imagine interviews, perhaps hiring some writer to prepare a book that would be published under Conklin's name. There would be speaking tours, possibly a fling at politics.

But first, he had to make it out of Siskiyou County alive.

Conklin had no interest in being listed with the victims murdered by a monstrous species, turned into a meal for something science had ignored and failed to catalog so far. His interviews and book, if he lived long enough, would have something to say about the great Smithsonian's techniques, and its pathetic representative who hid in camp, afraid, while real men faced the great, howling unknown.

Conklin might not have letters strung behind his name like Dr. Minninger, he might not be a cringing bureaucrat with friends in Washington like Abel Durst, but both had proved themselves unworthy of their role as "experts" in the present situation. Jake Shandy would reveal the truth, if he could get it printed—and if not, Conklin would take it to a bigger, better paper, like the *New York Times* or the *Chicago Tribune,* tell the story his way and make sure they got it right from the beginning.

He would be a hero if he made it back to Sacramento in one piece, and more so when he'd led a military expedition to eradicate the monsters that had brought his logging business to a standstill. Find the goddamned Missing Link and wipe it out, before it brought free trade in northern California to a grinding halt.

Hell, with that kind of press, Conklin might even run for President of the United States.

Careers had been founded on less, like that gangly rail-splitter out of Illinois. And Conklin wouldn't even need a civil war to win his place in history.

Omah would do it for him, on its short road to extinction, long since overdue.

Thorn regained his strength and the ability to breath again after he'd run for fifty yards or so along the game trail they had followed from the logging camp. His back still throbbed, and Thorn expected there would be an ugly bruise forming, but no bones had been broken and he was acquainted with the slow passage of pain. There'd be no sleeping on his back for several days, when this was over—and he knew that if he couldn't beat the top speed of the *Omah*s chasing him, sleep wouldn't matter any more.

His first attempt at talking mind-to-mind had failed, but Thorn was not discouraged yet. Battle was not the best time to communicate with anyone, human or animal, when both sides were intent on killing one another. He would try again, given a better opportunity, but in the meantime Thorn decided that his best hope for survival would be getting back to Yreka as soon as possible, with Bell and Shadow, to begin the railroad journey south.

He had one answer to the question that propelled him through his wanderings around the West: whatever *Omah* was, he could not blame it for the slaughter of his family when he was two years old. The size was right, at least approximately, but it did not have the fatal prowler's shaggy hair, and Thorn had seen first-hand that *Omah* lacked the long talons that killed his parents and his brother, leaving him with a memento on his scalp.

So *something else* was still his target, and while *Omah* posed another mystery, Thorn nurtured little hope of solving it himself—at least not on the Conklin expedition that was rapidly devolving into chaos.

They had two men dead, not counting lumberjacks he'd never met, and the "official" members of their team—from the Smithsonian and the Interior Department—were apparently disabled by their shock and fear at meeting predators beyond their understanding.

Welcome to my life, he thought, and almost smiled.

Siskiyou County held a mystery that Thorn would still enjoy unraveling, if it did not turn out to be the death of him, but at some other time. Perhaps *Omah* was known beyond Yreka and environs, through the northern half of California or even the entire Northwest. That was a question for another time, when Thorn had done his research thoroughly and had a better grasp of what awaited him.

Or maybe loggers would get there before him, hewing down the vast, majestic forest and eliminating any species in their path.

But not today.

The camp was closer now. Thorn smelled it, recognized the scent of humans and their buildings, open fires, even the slit trench slowly filling up with waste. A few more yards, with luck, and they would see—

A shriek sounded behind them, higher pitched than any of the giant *Omah*s had released so far, and Thorn spun in his tracks to find an Indian with long gray hair rushing along the game trail toward him, knife in one hand, while the other held a hatchet poised to strike.

Thorn had barely glimpsed the first attacker, when two more appeared, racing along the trail behind the old man who had shouted at him. As he turned, Migisi also pivoted, their rifles pointed back along the forest path to meet these unexpected enemies.

Migisi seemed to hesitate for just an instant, as the gray-haired hatchet-wielder closed the gap between them, letting go another high-pitched cry that put the capper on his obvious hostility. Thorn guessed it was the shock of firing on a fellow tribesman that delayed Migisi, but he felt no such restraint as he triggered a .44 into the old man's chest. Impact immediately broke the aged Indian's momentum and propelled him backward, sprawling supine with his arms outflung.

Behind him, the two younger warriors hesitated for a second, clearly startled by their leader's fall, then uttered war whoops of their own and charged ahead, leaping across the old man's corpse. Thorn just had time to see that one—the warrior on his left—was carrying a tomahawk, the other brandishing a knife. Apparently, they had learned nothing from their leader's folly in confronting guns with weapons that required personal contact.

Thorn had sighted on the nearest of the pair, was halfway through his trigger squeeze, when at his side, Migisi shot the warrior Thorn was aiming at, armed with the tomahawk. Shifting his stance, Thorn hoped the last survivor would think twice and turn to flee, but he continued his advance, raising another howl in hopes of terrifying his opponents.

He was barely six feet distant when Thorn shot him in the chest. The young man seemed to stumble, wallowed through a shoulder roll, and came to rest a yard in front of Thorn, his torso twisted at the waist, hands empty, fresh blood leaking through his buckskin shirt. Dead eyes stared at the distant sky, above the forest's looming trees.

Life seemed to freeze for one heartbeat, perhaps two, no sounds other than the echo of their gunshots audible, with silence settling over all. Thorn just had time to wonder if the *Omahs* had retreated, giving up the chase, when he saw movement farther back along the trail and heard the hunters' throaty growls.

Migisi turned and bolted toward the camp, with Thorn a pace or two behind him, closing in. Their stalkers seemed to hesitate upon encountering the warriors lying dead before them, but Thorn didn't stop to study their reaction. Anything that helped him gain a lead was welcome, and he planned on taking full advantage of it.

Suddenly, the logging camp came into view. It wasn't much, in terms of physical protection, as he'd learned the night before. But at that moment, in extremis, it appeared to be a fortress in the wilderness, hewn out of logs and populated by a group Thorn knew to be his comrades in the fight against *Omah.*

It was, in short, better than nothing.

As they reached the open courtyard of the camp, last night's fire long burned down to ash, Thorn and Migisi paused and turned to see how far their trackers would pursue them. None advanced beyond the treeline, but Thorn saw their shadows moving there and clearly heard the almost taunting cries they raised from hiding, as if calling out their enemies to join the fight.

Not yet, he thought, and trailed Migisi toward the camp's mess hall.

FIFTEEN

Armed loggers herded Thorn and his companion inside the mess hall, where they found the other three survivors of their woodland battle under care from Dr. Heaton. He was checking out Reginald Conklin's hip as best he could, the company vice president trying to walk with trousers down around his ankles, clearly mortified, while Heaton probed his bruise and Conklin's lumberjacks all made a point of looking elsewhere in the hall.

That wasn't difficult, since Ed Russell was holding forth about their skirmish in the woods, Jake Shandy wearing out another pencil as he captured pungent quotes and interspersed them with his own impressions of the fight. In another fairly isolated corner, Dr. Minninger and Abel Durst huddled together, still pale-faced and whispering to one another, like a pair of discontented ghosts.

More loggers soon surrounded Thorn, peppering him with questions, while Migisi was allowed to drift off toward a solitary corner and sit down, mostly ignored. Thorn cut the questions off as best he could, saying, "It's not important now, what happened in the woods. Those things were right behind us all the way, and now it's dark, we should expect more trouble anytime."

He made no mention of the three tribesmen who had attacked him and Migisi on the trail, fearing that revelation of that incident would turn the lumberjacks against Migisi in a lynching frenzy, fueled by their frustration over being penned inside the dining hall. The good news was, whatever food remained in camp was in the same location, so they wouldn't starve.

Being devoured was another question altogether.

And that danger was brought him a few short minutes later, by the fierce, almost demented howls outside. Full night had settled on the logging camp, and Thorn could almost feel the *Omah*s drawing closer, closing in around the dining hall that had become a makeshift fortress for the lumberjacks. He couldn't judge their numbers from the back-and-forth hooting and snarling, but the creatures' furious hostility was evident, both to his ears and to his mind.

That startled Thorn, the first real mental contact he'd achieved with any of the predators, and while he couldn't pin it down to any certain one of them, it still was *something.* As the loggers rushed to doors and boarded-over windows, bearing any weapons they possessed, Thorn took a moment for himself and bent his mind toward answering his enemies outside.

The talent he'd discovered as a child had served him well for many years, not only with his stallion and his mule, but also with assorted creatures of the wild. A few months back, while working on a job in Texas, he'd awakened to the pressure of a rattler coiled and sleeping on his chest. It took a while, but Thorn had managed to persuade the snake that it should crawl away, without sinking its fangs into his face.

Now, when his life was once again in jeopardy, Thorne reached out to the night as best he could, probing for any hint of receptivity among his enemies. Mental communication with another species did not feature verbal conversation in the normal sense, more a delivery of feelings via images and calming thoughts—which, in this case, failed to impress the *Omahs* that were fuming for revenge.

So be it. For the moment, there was nothing Thorn could do but fight.

Reginald Conklin was relieved to pull his pants up, hoist his black suspenders, and stop feeling like an utter fool. He looked to Dr. Heaton for a diagnosis, now more troubled by the howling from outside than by his private pain.

"You're badly bruised," the doctor said, "but nothing's broken."

"Good enough." He nodded toward the nearest door and said, "I guess you'll have your work cut out for you if *they* get in."

Heaton tried putting on a smile but couldn't manage it. "In that case," he replied, "I fear my services will be superfluous."

Conklin limped over to the place where Dr. Minninger and Abel Durst sat whispering. They both looked up at his approach and ceased conversing. Their stricken faces raised to his, the men reminded Conklin of dazed survivors he'd met after Wisconsin's Peshtigo Fire of 1871. Occurring on the same day as the fire that razed Chicago, Peshtigo's was already forgotten by most people living outside of the Badger State, though it had killed some fifteen hundred people—five times the toll from Chicago—and blackened more than eighteen hundred acres of virgin forest, leaving a wasteland twice the size of Rhode Island.

"What are you two doing over here?" he challenged them.

"Waiting," Durst said.

"For what?"

"For them to kill us," answered Minninger, his voice already sounding like a mutter from the grave.

"Jesus, that's it? You just give up and sit here waiting for those things break in here and slaughter all of us?"

"What can we do about it?" Minninger demanded, sounding angry now.

Conklin leaned toward him, made a fist, and rapped his knuckles sharply on the anthropologist's head. "Use *this.* Your brain. Washington sent you here because you were supposed to be some kind of expert."

Minninger gave out a gasping laugh at that. "Expert? Are you insane? Nobody's ever seen creatures like this before. There *are* no experts, Mr. Conklin. Only victims."

"So you're bloody useless, both of you? Is that your final word?"

Minninger flushed an angry pink but offered no reply. Durst hung his head, striking the pose of a regretful child caught stealing from his mother's cookie jar.

Disgusted, Conklin drew his pistol, cocked it, aiming at Minninger.

"So be it," he declared. "Useless it is, and I'll be damned if either one of you steal one more breath of air from the brave men preparing to defend us. Say your prayers, if you think God will listen to a pair of spineless cowards."

"Wait!" Durst raised a hand, as if it would deflect a bullet from his tear-streaked face. "I'll fight. I don't have any weapons, but—"

"And you?" Conklin demanded of the cringing anthropologist. "What will it be?"

"I'll play your game," said Minninger. "For all the good that it'll do."

"All right, then. On your feet and try to act like men. Find something, *anything* that you can fight with. I don't care if it's a fork or spoon. Be ready if they rush us. Don't disgrace yourselves in front of these brave men."

No sooner had he spoken, than a heavy stone landed atop the mess hall's roof. A moment later, they were falling like a summer downpour from the black night sky.

Migisi broke off praying when the stones began to fall. His ancestors had offered no advice of any value in his present situation, but he'd asked for them to bless him and to welcome him if, as he now expected without question, he should join them soon.

Cocking his Winchester, he looked around the mess hall and saw loggers manning all the doors and windows. Those with guns were at the forefront, others armed with axes, picks, and other tools stood close behind them, ready to jump in and strike if the front-line defense was breached.

Migisi did not join them, knowing in advance that he would be unwelcome in their ranks, a lowly "redskin" trying to intrude. Some of the lumberjacks probably blamed him, as a Yurok, for the deadly threat they faced. Their fear and superstition—be they French, German, whatever—likely had at least a few of them believing rumors that *Omah* was conjured by a Yurok shaman to remove whites from the Shasta Cascade region and preserve the tribe's ancestral hunting grounds. If he approached them now...

The thought of shamans took Migisi back to the attack he suffered with the white man, Thorn, as they retreated toward the logging camp. Thorn had killed the gray-haired Yurok, far too old to be a chosen warrior, and Migisi had joined in to finish off the old man's two young braves. Did that make him a traitor to his people, as some already accused, since he'd agreed to serve the white men as a guide?

It was too late to worry about such things now. Migisi's fate was sealed, he thought, depending on what happened next. If *Omah* simply stoned the mess hall, as they had the night before, and then retreated to the wild, he might survive. In that case, he'd decided that he would depart from camp next morning, never mind the pay that he was owed, and try to find someplace where he was known to no one and could pass unnoticed, maybe make a living guiding hunters now and then, without arousing angry Yuroks or *Omah*. Perhaps he'd even leave the state, or at the very least, try eking out a living to the south, around the growing village of Los Angeles.

But if the *Omah*s forced their way inside the dining hall...

Perhaps he just had time for one more prayer, asking his ancestors to give him strength, resolve, and let him face whatever happened in the next few minutes like a true warrior of old. Migisi had faced rival tribesmen in his time, along with savage bears and mountain lions, but the thought of fighting *Omah* hand to giant hand unnerved him.

Above all, he must not show fear before the lumberjacks

who held him in disdain. That shame would follow him into the Spirit World and taint him for eternity.

If all else failed, Migisi vowed to stand and die with courage.

What else could he do?

"This is absurd," said Theo Minninger to Abel Durst. "We're not soldiers. What does that madman think the two of us can do?"

"Stand up and face whatever's coming," Durst replied, fresh resignation in his voice.

"We should be getting out of here."

"Oh, yes? And how do you propose to do that, *Doctor?*"

That stumped Minninger. His fear had overcome him, but in fact, he had no earthly notion as to how escape from the mess hall, much less the logging camp, could be accomplished in full darkness, with those savage *things* surrounding it.

The kitchen knife that he was clutching would not stop one of the monsters, though it briefly crossed his mind that he could use it on himself and end this nightmare before things got any worse. Given the choice of that or being eaten up alive, it was no choice at all.

"We need a rifle," Minninger announced.

"Oh, yes?" Durst answered, clearly mocking him. "Just look around. They're taken, if you hadn't noticed."

"When the fighting starts again, we'll have a chance to grab one."

"*Grab* one? Do you think whoever's using it will simply give it up?"

Minninger raised his knife. "We won't give him a choice."

Durst actually laughed at that, a jarring sound. "Of course. And if the others don't just shoot us down, then what?"

"The backdoor," Minninger replied. "Go out that way and run like hell to reach the stable."

"While the monsters stand and watch? You've lost your mind."

"Last time, they focused on the front doors and the windows," Minninger reminded him. "Most of the lumberjacks are there, as you can see."

"Most, but not all."

"*Enough* of them. While they're engaged in holding off these things, we make our move. Taking a rifle's just a moment's work, and then we're out before they have a chance to stop us."

Durst stared at Minninger, as if he'd grown a second head. It seemed as if the bureaucrat could not decide whether to laugh or cry. It took another moment for him to respond, at which time he said, "No."

"No, what?"

"I'm saying no to all of it. I won't help you attack one of the loggers for his weapon, and I will not go outside with you on some fool's errand. If we have a chance at all, it's here, inside."

"And you call *me* a fool?" Minninger spat at him. "So be it. I'll be halfway to Yreka when those monsters start picking their teeth with your bones."

Durst paled, but found the strength to answer back, "I doubt that very much."

That said, he rose and moved away from Minninger, leaving the anthropologist alone. Stones were cascading down upon the mess hall now, rolling across its sloped roof and rebounding from its sturdy walls. One of the makeshift window shutters took a heavy hit and sprouted cracks, but did not burst inward—so far.

Minninger gripped the steak knife tight enough to make his knuckles crack, wondering whether he possessed the fortitude to use it on a man, if that was what it took to save his life. And if he did...what then?

Rising, he started moving slowly toward the dining hall's backdoor, where only two men had been left on guard.

Thorn stepped in front of Conklin as the lumberman returned to join his loggers massed around the dining hall's front doors and windows. Conklin blinked, seeming surprised to see him, as if he'd forgotten Thorn was there.

"Excuse me, Mr. Thorn. I—"

"It's important that you hear me out," Thorn interrupted him. "I think there's still a way to salvage this."

"And that would be...?"

"Surrender," Thorn replied.

"*Surrender?*" Conklin gaped at him. "Should we all throw our weapons down, open the doors, and welcome them inside?"

"No, sir. We need to leave and let them know that we're not coming back. *You* need to let them know. Suspend the local logging operation."

"Are you mad? Did one of those rocks strike you on the head?"

"I know it's hard to grasp the fact, but your employees have been trespassing."

"Nonsense! I paid good money for this timberland, arranged it all in Washington, through proper channels. Leaders of the Yuroks had their say, and they were overruled. The courts have settled it."

Thorn nodded toward the nearby double doors. "Those aren't Yuroks out there. And they don't recognize the rulings of a court, much less one on the far side of the continent. They're fighting for their homeland and their future. Can you understand that?"

"Christ, Thorn! These are *animals!*"

"What do you know about the great apes, Mr. Conklin? Very little, I suspect."

"Great apes? You mean in Africa and Borneo? I don't have time for—"

"This is all the time you *do* have," Thorn corrected him. "These *Omah,* call them what you will, resemble us and, I believe, possess some mechanism to communicate. Imagine taking on a tribe of furious gorillas, only larger, better organized."

"See here—"

"So far, they've beaten us at every turn. They're stronger, know the country better, and are not afraid to die."

"They don't have guns."

"Ours haven't helped us much, so far," Thorn said.

Conklin stood glaring at him for another moment, then asked, "What is it you'd have me do?"

"Tell them that you'll be shutting down and pulling out. Look elsewhere for your lumber. There'd no shortage that I've seen so far, from Sacramento up to Canada."

"Surrender to a bunch of *animals*." Conklin was clearly fuming, furious at the idea. When I've crushed men who tried to thwart my will."

"A wise man knows his limitations," Thorn advised. "That demonstrates intelligence, not cowardice."

"You take a lot for granted, sir. What if these things don't understand a word I say? What if they just don't give a damn? They have us penned up here like sheep. Why let us leave the camp alive?"

"I don't plan to communicate with words," Thorn said.

Conklin leaned closer to him. "I require an explanation of that extraordinary statement."

"If you'd only trust—"

A cry from the backdoor cut short Thorn's answer. Turning, both men saw a logger lying curled up on the floor, clutching his stomach. Theo Minninger stood over him, holding a Winchester and fending off the other guard, who held an axe.

Before he could be stopped, the anthropologist opened the door, bolted outside, and vanished in the howling night.

SIXTEEN

Theo Minninger amazed himself. At first, he hadn't thought that he possessed the nerve to brace a pair of armed men with a simple kitchen knife, much less succeed, but he had managed it, against all odds. The fresh blood on his right hand, where he'd jammed the blade into one logger's abdomen, repulsed him, but he'd done the job: disarmed the wounded rifleman as he was falling, dropped the bloody knife beside his victim, and then aimed the rifle at the second lumberjack whose axe was no match for a Winchester.

The rest was simple, once his blood was up, as some people might say. Of course, the axe man cried out in alarm, but he made no move to prevent Minninger from opening the backdoor, lunging through it into noisy darkness, and escaping from the barricaded dining hall.

The anthropologist had started having second thoughts an instant later, when the door was slammed and barred behind him, shutting out the night and all its terrors. Part of him knew he was better off without damned Abel Durst, the yellow-bellied office rat who lacked both the initiative and nerve to save himself.

It struck Minninger now that he'd become a criminal, perhaps a murderer, but that thought was succeeded swiftly by another: *Omah,* in its rage and hunger, would erase the evidence and any witnesses. Minninger's only task now was to reach the stable, find a horse, and ride like hell away from camp, if he could manage it.

One huge and overwhelming *if.*

He heard the beasts howling behind him, pressing their attack upon the dining hall, but he could also tell that one or more of them were coming after him, presumably intent on letting no one get away. Steeling himself, he turned and looked back toward the mess hall, where he saw not one, but two tall shadows jogging in pursuit of him.

Minninger's knowledge of the rifle he had stolen from the man he'd stabbed was minimal—only that it was cocked, the hammer back, thus should be loaded and prepared to fire. He raised it to his shoulder, sighting hastily along the barrel, and squeezed off a shot before he'd braced himself for the recoil. The butt plate struck his shoulder, jarring him, and Minninger immediately knew that he had missed both predators, although the noise and muzzle flash had slowed them down.

Were they afraid? Could such things even grasp a sense of fear?

Minninger wasted precious seconds staring at the stolen rifle, then went through the necessary motions with its lever-action to eject an empty cartridge and replace it with a fresh one in the chamber. How many remained? His mind was blank on that as Minninger aimed once again, this time holding his breath, leaning into the rifle, centering its sights as well as he could manage on the nearer of the two advancing monsters.

This time, when the weapon kicked, it did not take him by surprise. What *did* was seeing his selected target stagger, clutching its broad chest with both huge hands, and tumble to the ground. It's fierce companion hesitated, bending down and peering at the stricken one, no longer howling in its rage.

Minninger swallowed down a hoot of triumph, turning from the monster he had shot, and ran.

Thorn gave no thought to chasing after Dr. Minninger. Wherever he was going with the weapon he had stolen, Gideon supposed that fleeing from the mess hall virtually guaranteed his death. As Dr. Heaton rushed to aid the wounded lumberjack, Thorn turned back to the door and windows that were under fierce attack.

The loggers, some two-thirds of them, were massed along that wall with Conklin shouting orders at them, doing everything they could to brace the dining hall's weak points against invasion by the horde outside. The savage howls and roars made it impossible for Thorn to estimate how many *Omah*s had the place surrounded. Fewer than the number of men trapped inside, he guessed, but since each one of them was two or three feet taller than a large man, also many times stronger, only the logger's firearms gave them any hope at all of living through the night.

And after that? What was to stop the creatures keeping up their siege by daylight, until they had broken in and massacred the humans they despised?

Nothing.

Again, despite the racket both inside and outside of the dining hall, Thorn reached out with his mind, hoping that one or more of the attackers might respond somehow. He felt his thoughts connecting, penetrating, but the storm of fury that consumed his adversaries masked any potential answer from outside.

For all he knew, this species was immune to any powers he possessed, as Thorn had found with certain birds—and, for that matter, human beings. He had never tried communicating with another breed of primate, and was on the verge of giving up, joining the lumberjacks to fight until he died, when something tickled lightly in his head—a thought, perhaps, that was not his.

When trying to communicate with other species silently, Thorn did not frame his thoughts in human speech. Rather, he generally tried projecting calm, a sense of understanding, and an openness to any thoughts the other creature might exchange with him. If such thoughts were received, they generally came to Thorn as images—of food, the animal's surroundings, any cause for fear—and he would try his best to placate fright, hostility, the negative emotions that precipitated conflict.

Now, beyond the wall of rage, he felt an urgency demanding Thorn and all those like him to depart from Conklin's logging camp and from the area at large. Together with it, he received an image of the loggers leaving, watched by shadow figures in the forest, keeping track of them but not attacking as they made an orderly retreat.

Or was that only Thorn's own wishful thinking?

Spotting Conklin as he moved along the line of tired defenders, Thorn felt a compulsion to accost the man and try once more to reason with him. If the killing could be ended, and the rest of his employees saved from harm, was it not worth abandoning the site? Thorn was no businessman—accountants back in Boston kept a close eye on his fortune, overseen by loyal Obi Magoro—but he recognized the greed that drove some men of capital to grasp for every penny they could reach until they were, themselves, destroyed.

If Conklin proved to be that single-minded, that irrational, then all of them were doomed. But otherwise, if he would only *listen*...

As Conklin passed him, Thorn reached out to grip his arm.

Surprised, Conklin rounded on Stone, his free hand reaching for the pistol tucked under his belt. "What do you want?" he challenged. "Can't you see I'm *busy,* for Christ's sake?"

"You need to listen," Thorn replied. "I can't explain this to you in the time we have, but I'm convinced these things will let us—all your people—live, if you agree to leave the camp.

"Not that, again!" Conklin spat at him. "Do you know how mad you sound? Talking to *animals* and hoping they'll respond? And if it works, what then? Pissing a fortune down a rat hole and explaining to the board, to our investors, why we walked away from timber valued in the millions? It's insane."

"You'd rather die tonight, with all your men, and have whoever's sent to tidy up the mess you've made walk into the same thing, repeating your mistakes?"

Conklin considered that, then caught himself about to weaken and replied, "I can't. These men would think I've lost my mind. They'd laugh, if they weren't terrified, and when I fail, they'd never listen to another word I say. Nobody in his right mind would."

"Is *that* what you're afraid of? Looking foolish? Would you really rather die than have a group of men you barely know wonder about your sanity? And if it works..."

"It won't."

"But *if it does,* you've saved them all. Do you imagine the survivors will dispute your methods then?"

Conklin felt like an idiot as he replied, "If I accept that, what exactly should I do?"

"Say what I told you, in your own words. Call out loud enough to make it heard, and *mean* it. If you doubt yourself or think of tricking them, they'll see through any lies you tell and press home the attack."

"My reputation..."

"You can either be the man who stopped this, saving lives, or you can be remembered as a man who died while fighting bravely. Would you rather live or die?"

"But you can't guaranteed this will succeed?"

"No," Thorn replied. "There are no guarantees. But if it fails, we still die all the same. What have you got to lose? There'll be no witnesses to mock you, afterward."

Conklin swallowed and tried to put his thoughts in order, weighing pros and cons as more stones slammed against the dining hall and hulking creatures threw their weight against the doors. At last, he turned from Thorn to face his lumberjacks, dragooned as soldiers in a fight they could not hope to win.

"Men!" Conklin shouted to them. "Listen up! There's something that I want to try, and I need quiet from the rest of you."

The frightened lumberjacks slowly quit jabbering

among themselves, most turning toward their boss, a few still angling weapons toward the doors and shuttered windows. When he had their full attention, Conklin forged ahead.

"All right. I don't have time to argue this with any of you, so I'll just say that we have a plan—that's Mr. Thorn and I—" sharing the blame, at least, "—to stop this lunacy and get you out of here alive. No matter what I do or say, the rest of you must listen and *be quiet.* Anyone who speaks out while I'm talking jeopardizes what we hope to do, and just might kill us all."

That silenced any muttering among the loggers. Ed Russell, their foreman, asked his boss, "What should we do, sir?"

"First, pull down the plywood from that window—no, be quiet now and hear me out! Open the shutter on that window and step back. Just watch and listen, without interrupting me."

Thorn chimed in then, saying, "And keep your minds at ease, if you can manage it."

Before that could be questioned, Conklin said. "All right, then. Do it now. And if I fail you, boys, I want to say I'm sorry in advance. At least you know I'll pay for it."

Theo Minninger had reached the stable when he realized the bestial howling had begun to taper off, its echoes dying down. He risked a glance back toward the dining hall, saw nothing trailing him, and wondered if the monsters had already breached the building and were busy feasting on the men inside.

No matter.

All Minninger cared about was putting miles between himself and the accursed logging camp. If all the witnesses to his impulsive crime were slain, so much the better. No one would dispute the contents of his field report to the Smithsonian—a document which he believed would be officially suppressed and hidden from the populace at large until such time as humans could accept the eerie, brutal truth.

Around the twelfth of Never, he supposed.

He crept into the stable, one lamp burning on a wall hook, with its wick turned low. Minninger knew which horse he wanted, had been wishing it was his since he'd first seen Gideon Thorn leading his stallion from the railroad stock car in Yreka. Now he found the gray inside its stall, watching him with suspicious eyes as he approached. Beside it, on its left, was Thorn's pack mule.

"Hello, boy," Minninger addressed the horse. "We're going for a little ride. Your master won't be coming with us, sad to say. But *I'm* your master now."

The stallion's saddle sat atop the door that kept it penned inside its stall, reins looped around the saddle's horn. Minninger cleared the latch, opened the door, and stepped into the stall that smelled of hay and dung.

"Good boy. Just calm yourself. The bad things seem to have their hands and mouths fill at the moment."

Helplessly, unconsciously, Minninger giggled at his own sick joke.

And he was setting down the stolen Winchester, turning to lift Thorn's saddle from its perch, when Shadow reared behind him, rising on its hind legs without any sound or warning, lashing out with his front hooves.

The blow struck Theo Minninger's skull like a hatchet, splitting bone, and slammed his face against the stall's rough door as he pitched forward, down and down into the depths of darkness everlasting.

Gideon Thorn was half surprised himself, when Conklin's promise, shouted through the mess hall's open window to the night, cut through the angry howling and suppressed it to a murmur from the dark. Some of the lumberjacks inside looked stunned, others relieved, but all of them kept silent as they had been ordered, standing with their weapons poised in case one of the creatures snatched their boss man through the window and the killing raid resumed.

Thorn, for his part, stood with his fingers crossed, hoping.

He could not tell if Conklin was sincere, unable as he was to read another human's mind or heart, but something in the lumberman's expressive tone apparently had reached the *Omahs* gathered in the darkness that surrounded them. Whatever they were thinking now—and Thorn couldn't be sure, the images that came to his mind being jumbled, contradictory—at least, if only for a moment, they were *listening*.

And what then, if they managed to *believe*?

He wondered about Theo Minninger, whether the lull in bloodlust had occurred in time to save him, where he planned to go and how he hoped to get there, how he would explain his stabbing of the logger whose Winchester Minninger had stolen. Those were all the doctor's problems now, of course, and Thorn could only wish him all the luck he felt that Minninger deserved as things played out.

Which wasn't much.

"I think they're leaving!" Conklin's voice cut through

Thorn's contemplation. Several of the loggers crowded closer, trying for a view outside through Conklin's window, then another one was opened on the far side of the double doors.

"He's right!" somebody said. "I see 'em going! There, and there!"

Thorn didn't try to catch a glimpse of the retreating creatures. He was satisfied to take it in and feel himself beginning to relax—until a sudden thought intruded on his feeling of relief. If Minninger was planning to escape the camp, he'd need a ride, and that meant stopping by the stable first, to steal a horse.

Guards on the backdoor thought of stopping Thorn but gave it up when they saw the expression on his face. Outside, he paused to smell the night, still redolent with *Omah*'s heavy musk, then struck off toward the stable on the path he guessed that Dr. Minninger had followed, if he got that far.

Thorn found no human corpse along the way, but saw blood glistening on grass at one point. Was it Minninger's, or had the anthropologist managed to wound a prowling creature as he fled? Thorn looked more closely, searching for the rifle *Omah* would have left abandoned at the scene while killing Minninger, and found no weapon there, before he ran on toward the stable.

There, the wide door stood ajar, where someone or something had entered. Thorn experienced a sudden flash of fear for Bell and Shadow, then he felt their minds touch his, before he stepped inside. A solitary lamp provided light enough for Thorn to make out what had happened there, while Conklin was negotiating with the forest monsters from the dining hall.

Whatever Minninger had planned, in terms of an

escape, his scheme had gone awry when he chose Shadow as his mount. Sprawled on the bloody hay, brains leaking from his shattered skull, the coward had run out of time and luck.

Thorn dragged him clear, then soothed his animal companions, offering them extra food to take their minds off blood and death. That done, he left them with a parting word, secured the stable door, and started back in the direction of the mining hall.

SEVENTEEN

YREKA: APRIL 25, 1876

Evacuation of a logging camp, however minimal its furnishings, took time, and Thorn was not inclined to wait around until the final lumberjacks pulled out. He left after a hasty breakfast, Monday morning, and returned the way he'd come with Bell and Shadow, to Yreka, watching all the way for any shadows following behind him. None appeared, but he was still relieved to reach his destination and discover rooms available at the Yreka's Rest hotel.

Thorn had expected troubled sleep that night, before he caught the southbound train on Tuesday, but he was surprised to pass the night without a single dream that he recalled. He kept his weapons handy while he slept, but never reached for them or jerked awake from nightmares of the forest-dwelling creatures that had claimed so many lives.

What were they? Thorn still had no answers, and decided he would leave it to the scientists who followed up on Conklin's story of the incident. Perhaps they would be made of stronger stuff than Theo Minninger, but would their presence spark another woodland murder spree?

If so, Thorn wouldn't be around to witness it. Despite the glaring questions that remained, he knew one thing beyond all doubt: *Omah* was not the creature that had torn his family apart and left him with the scar atop his head as a reminder of the massacre. Whatever he was seeking, whether for revenge or simple satisfaction of his curiosity, it had been something else—something as yet unknown.

His train was scheduled to leave at half-past ten o'clock, which left Thorn ample time for breakfast at the hotel's nearly-empty restaurant. He ordered steak and eggs, with fried potatoes, mushrooms, toast, and black coffee, happy to wait his turn until the meal arrived.

"May I join you?"

The sound of Conklin's voice surprised him. Thorn had guessed the lumberman would still be at the forest campsite, seeing it dismantled to his satisfaction.

"You left early," he observed, as Conklin sat down facing him, across the table.

"Russell has it all in hand," Conklin replied. "I came back yesterday, not long after you left us. Abel Durst and Dr. Heaton, too. I'd guess we'll all be riding back to Sacramento on the morning train."

Thorn nodded, thanked the waitress as his steaming plate arrived, while Conklin ordered scrambled eggs and ham. "Don't wait for me," the logger said. "I wouldn't want your breakfast getting cold."

While Thorn dug in, he asked, "How do you think your board will take the news you're shutting down the camp?"

"About that," Conklin said. "I wired headquarters yesterday, as soon as we got back. I'll have to make a full report in person, naturally, but ... I'm not sure if they'll go for it."

Thorn pinned him with a stare and said, "Explain."

"You have to see their side of it. The forest in this range can make them—make *us*—millions. To abandon it, just pull up stakes and leave, will send a major shock wave through the company and, frankly, anger its investors."

"So?" Thorn challenged. "Would they rather be angry, or dead?"

"You must know the executives and stockholders will never come within a hundred miles of Siskiyou. Their first concern is profits—or, for the investors, healthy dividends. All else is ... secondary."

"Jesus, man, you gave your word!"

"I did, but try to see it from the corporate perspective, Mr. Thorn. What does it mean to give your word *to animals?* My God, it sounds insane to even say the words aloud in daylight, sitting here."

"It's all that saved out lives on Sunday night."

"Perhaps," said Conklin, nodding. "I saw all the same things that you did, of course. It *seemed* that what I said convinced those...things...to let us go in peace, but honestly..."

Thorn nearly laughed at Conklin's choice of words. "The *honest* thing would be to keep your promise," he replied.

"And I'd be happy to, if it were only up to me."

"The company again."

"Of course. My title is Vice President of Operations. Mr. Thorn, if I don't *operate,* if I refuse to follow orders from my own superiors, how long do you suppose I'd keep that job? How long before they find someone who's willing to obey their orders and proceed with logging in the Siskiyou?"

"But—"

Conklin raised a hand to silence Thorn. "I will discuss this seriously with the board in Sacramento and explain—*try* to explain—why I believe we should relocate operations elsewhere. As to whether they will listen...well, I'd say that is unlikely."

"Fools."

"They haven't seen what we did," Conklin said. "Perhaps, when I describe it, they will understand, but realistically..." He let the sentence trail away just as the waitress brought his plate and mug of coffee.

"Then more men will die. You *know* they will."

"In fact, from what I read last night—the wire from headquarters, in answer to my own—the board may choose to clear the woods before logging resumes."

"And what does *that* mean?" Even asking it, Thorn worried that he might already know.

"More hunters, I suspect," Conklin replied, "and plenty of them, this time. I imagine they could flush these creatures out and deal with them. If the Yuroks cause any problems...well, there's still the army, isn't there? I spoke to Mr. Durst, and after what he's seen, I'm guessing that some kind of quiet intervention by the government may be arranged."

"A 'quiet intervention'? What you mean is wiping out the species."

Conklin shrugged. "I'd have no part in planning tactics, much less executing them. But think about it, Mr. Thorn: a species that we've never seen before, which has no benefit to man. Perhaps exterminating them would be a favor to the world."

Thorn did laugh, then. "A favor? And suppose they

don't oblige you, Mr. Conklin. Then, what? Are you ready for a war and the publicity that comes with it?"

"As to publicity, my company has influence with every major newspaper on the West Coast—and with others far removed. Suppressing news of any 'war,' as you describe it, should be relatively simple, with the State Department's aid from Washington."

"Jake Shandy—"

"Will be in for a surprise, I gather, when he starts to write his story for the *Chronicle*. They love a scoop but live in fear of being made to look like raving idiots."

"So, they'd just bury it?"

"It wouldn't be the first time inconvenient news was swept under a rug."

"And Shandy? Will he swallow that?"

"He's not a fool. Unless he wants to find a new career, he won't buck major editors and publishers to push a story no one's likely to believe, regardless."

Thorn glanced at his plate and found that he had lost his appetite. Conklin, meanwhile, was forking down his eggs and ham like they were going out of style.

"So, tell me this," Thorn said. "Can you live with yourself it you send loggers back to face what we went through up there?"

"You heard me say the district would be cleared?"

"I heard you. And I don't believe it for a second. You saw how those creatures are. They lie back, waiting, and they choose their time to strike."

"I readily admit they're cunning," Conklin answered. "But they're still just *animals*. You make them sound like seasoned warriors, when there's nothing to suggest—"

"Have you stopped trusting your own eyes and ears?"

Conklin leaned forward, elbows on the table now, his

voice dropped closer to a whisper. "I was *frightened,* Mr. Thorn. I did what you suggested in the moment, what I thought was necessary, to preserve our lives. But now, as I reflect upon the matter—"

"On the profit margin, don't you mean?"

"It's *business.* A man of your resources understands the concept, yes? Boardroom decisions are not made based on some kind of tribal 'medicine' or voodoo."

"Voodoo's from New Orleans," Thorn replied. "And we weren't fighting native medicine in Siskiyou. Those creatures were alive and thinking through their every move."

"It might have seemed that way..."

"You know better than that!"

Conklin sat back and spread his hands. "I'll do my best when meeting with the board. You have my word on that."

"And what's that worth, exactly?"

Conklin's cheeks flushed pink. "You have to reason to insult me, sir."

"Insult you? I'm just pointing out the facts. You've said your word means nothing when you offer it to *animals.* Why should a stranger who you'll never see again be any different?"

"Because I mean to keep it! But I'd be a liar if I said the final choice was mine. It isn't, and it never will be while I'm just vice president."

"Why even bother, then?"

"Because I don't want any more lives on my conscience, damn it! I could quit in protest, try to find another job somewhere, but what would that accomplish?"

"If you couple it with putting out the word, it might do something," Thorn replied.

"The papers won't take my word, any more than they'll take Shandy's. By the time the government got through with me, I'd be a hopeless laughingstock. I might end up in an asylum."

"What about the scientists from the Smithsonian? They must be interested, wondering about what happened to their anthropologist."

"He died," Conklin replied. "A tragic accident, that's all. Killed by a horse—*your* horse, in fact—not by some mountain monster."

"But—"

"Please, Mr. Thorn: be sensible. The grand Smithsonian is staffed by scientists but overseen by bureaucrats. They follow orders, just like everybody else in government, and they depend on annual appropriations. There's no future there for anyone in spreading crazy campfire tales around."

"So it was all for nothing."

"On the contrary. If I receive the orders I'm expecting from my board, the forest will be cleansed of those abominable pests, and profitable logging will proceed. The Yuroks have the same choice that they've had since Europeans first discovered California. They can go along, or else."

"More 'cleansing' of the forest."

"Making way for progress. You've read history. When was it ever any different?"

"I keep hoping."

"Ah. You are an idealist. Which brings me to a question, if I may?"

"Go on."

"You came to California seeking information on what happened to your family. Was it of any use to you?"

"Another dead end," Thorn replied.

"Regrettable. But now you can move on, look elsewhere, unencumbered by the memory of Siskiyou County."

"You think so?"

"I devoutly *hope* so. I'll be trying to forget it for a long time, I suspect."

"But forging on ahead, as if it never happened."

"Not quite. Next time, if there is a next time, all precautions will be taken."

"And you hope that it will be enough."

"We live in hope, eh?"

"Or avoid the pitfalls that we know can bring us down."

"I envy you," said Conklin. "Free to roam around the country as you please, leading a life of mystery and high adventure. If I were a younger man myself, a different kind of man, perhaps I'd do the same. But as it is..."

"The money won't let you escape."

"That's easy said, when you're already set for life."

"The money helps," Thorn granted. "But I'd still be doing this, regardless of my family inheritance."

"If you say so," Conklin replied. "In any case, I'm *not* a young adventurer, merely a businessman of middle age who can't afford to toss his whole life on the rubbish heap. If you condemn me for it, that's a burden I can live with."

"And the deaths?"

"The company will compensate their families."

"I mean the deaths to come," Thorn said. "How many will it take, before your board begins to understand they can't just bulldoze nature and expect to get away with it?"

"Why not? It's happening all over, coast to coast. A hundred years from now, I doubt there'll be a virgin forest standing anywhere in the United States. Logging's required for all kinds of construction: homes, commercial properties, government buildings—take your pick."

"And when there's nothing left?"

"No monsters," Conklin said. "No place for them to hide. That ought to please you, Mr. Thorn."

Without another word, Thorn dropped his napkin on the table, rose, and left his meal unfinished on the plate. He was afraid that if he lingered any longer, it would take half of the hotel's staff to drag him off the lumberman, and what good would he be to anyone in jail? Better to bide his time, get on his scheduled train, and see what he could do in Sacramento—or, perhaps, in San Francisco, if he couldn't catch Jake Shandy sooner.

At the same time, Thorn saw bitter truth in what Conklin had said. People, especially in government, were prone to hiding awkward, inconvenient facts. In his own case, the slaughter of his family, a local lawman had dismissed the slayings as an animal attack—a bear, no less, that had forgotten how to hibernate and then had suffered an attack of pity after killing three humans, to spare a two-year-old.

People believed what it was helpful to believe, whatever let them go about their daily lives without obsessive worry over the unknown. Life in the latter nineteenth century held trials enough for any man or woman, without adding excess mystery and fear into the mix.

Thorn reckoned that he would be glad to see the last of California, at least for now. He would avoid the great north woods in future...unless something drew him back again, that is, to seek the answers he was always looking for.

And even if that happened, he would definitely shy away from Siskiyou. A promise made, in his mind, was a promise to be kept. *Omah* might blame him with the rest, if Conklin broke his word, and that was all the more reason to stay out of the monster's reach. Not running—Thorn was not a coward—but if he could only honor his part of the promise by avoiding future contact with the *Omah,* that would have to be enough.

He set off walking toward the livery, to check on Bell and Shadow, make sure they were ready for another journey on the train. From Sacramento, Thorn would ride—eastward, perhaps, or maybe to the south. Mysteries waited for him everywhere, regardless of the compass point he chose. And there was no time like the present to begin.

A LOOK AT SOUL SLAYERS (GIDEON THORN BOOK 5)

BY MICHAEL NEWTON

While potential news related to his family's murder makes its way from Colorado Territory to Boston, and on from there to find him somewhere in the West, Gideon Thorn confronts his greatest challenge yet: trying to solve and end a brutal string of mutilation murders in southern California, before the men--or things--responsible complete their dark design and usher in a new millennium of horror on Earth.

AVAILABLE JANUARY 2026

ABOUT THE AUTHOR

A California native, Michael Newton published over 215 books under his own name and various pseudonyms since 1977. He began writing professionally as a "ghost" for author Don Pendleton on the best-selling Executioner series. With 104 episodes published to date, Newton nearly tripled the number of Mack Bolan novels completed by creator Pendleton himself.

www.ingramcontent.com/pod-product-compliance
Lightning Source LLC
LaVergne TN
LVHW090514110826
845146LV00003B/858

9798895679388